THE KALAHARI TYPING SCHOOL FOR MEN

THE KALAHARI
TYPING SCHOOL FOR MEN

Alexander McCall Smith

Alfred A. Knopf Canada

National Library of Canada Cataloguing in Publication

McCall Smith, R. A.
The Kalahari typing school for men : more from the No. 1 Ladies'
Detective Agency / Alexander McCall Smith.

(No. 1 Ladies' Detective Agency)
Co-published by Pantheon Books.
ISBN 0-676-97568-2

I. Title. II. Series.

PR6063.C326K35 2003   823'.914   C2002-904787-0

First Edition
www.randomhouse.ca
Printed and bound in the United States of America
10 9 8 7 6 5 4 3 2 1

This book is for
Amy Moore
Florence Christie
and
Elaine Gadd

THE KALAHARI TYPING SCHOOL FOR MEN

CHAPTER ONE

HOW TO FIND A MAN

I MUST REMEMBER, thought Mma. Ramotswe, how fortunate I am in this life; at every moment, but especially now, sitting on the verandah of my house in Zebra Drive, and looking up at the high sky of Botswana, so empty that the blue is almost white. Here she was then, Precious Ramotswe, owner of Botswana's only detective agency, The No. 1 Ladies' Detective Agency—an agency which by and large had lived up to its initial promise to provide satisfaction for its clients, although some of them, it must be said, could never be satisfied. And here she was too, somewhere in her late thirties, which as far as she was concerned was the very finest age to be; here she was with the house in Zebra Drive and two orphan children, a boy and a girl, bringing life and chatter into the home. These were blessings with which anybody should be content. With these things in one's life, one might well say that nothing more was needed.

But there was more. Some time ago, Mma. Ramotswe had become engaged to Mr. J.L.B. Matekoni, proprietor of Tlokweng Road Speedy Motors, and by all accounts the finest mechanic in Botswana, a kind man, and a gentle one. Mma. Ramotswe had been married once before, and the experience had been disastrous. Note Mokoti, the smartly dressed jazz trumpeter, might have been a young girl's dream, but he soon turned out to be a wife's nightmare. There had been a daily diet of cruelty, of hurt given out like a ration, and when, after her fretful pregnancy, their tiny, premature baby had died in her arms, so few hours after it had struggled into life, Note had been off drinking in a shebeen somewhere. He had not even come to say good-bye to the little scrap of humanity that had meant so much to her and so little to him. When at last she left Note, Mma. Ramotswe would never forget how her father, Obed Ramotswe, whom even today she called the Daddy, had welcomed her back and had said nothing about her husband, not once saying I knew this would happen. And from that time she had decided that she would never again marry unless—and this was surely impossible—she met a man who could live up to the memory of the late Daddy, that fine man whom everybody respected for his knowledge of cattle and for his understanding of the old Botswana ways.

Naturally there had been offers. Her old friend Hector Mapondise had regularly asked her to marry him, and although she had just as regularly declined, he had always taken her refusals in good spirit, as befitted a man of his status (he was a cousin of a prominent chief). He would have made a perfectly good husband, but the problem was that he was rather dull and, try as she might, Mma. Ramotswe could scarcely prevent herself from nodding off in his company. It would be very difficult being married to him; a somnolent experience, in fact, and Mma. Ramotswe enjoyed life too much to want to sleep through it. Whenever she saw Hector Mapondise driving past in his large green car, or walking to the post office to collect his mail, she remembered the occasion on which he had taken her to lunch at the President Hotel and she had fallen asleep at the table, halfway through the meal. It had given a new meaning, she reflected, to the expression *sleeping with a man*. She had woken, slumped back in her chair, to see him staring at her with his slightly rheumy eyes, still talking in his low voice about some difficulty he was having with one of the machines at his factory.

"Corrugated iron is not easy to handle," he was saying. "You need very special machines to push the iron into that shape. Do you know that, Mma. Ramotswe? Do you know why corrugated iron is the shape it is?"

Mma. Ramotswe had not thought about this. Corrugated iron was widely used for roofing: was it, then, something to do with providing ridges for the rain to run off? But why would that be necessary in a dry country like Botswana? There must be some other reason, she imagined, although it was not immediately apparent to her. The thought of it, however, made her feel drowsy again, and she struggled to keep her eyes open.

No, Hector Mapondise was a worthy man, but far too dull. He should seek out a dull woman, of whom there were legions throughout the country, women who were slow-moving and not very exciting, and he should marry one of these bovine ladies. But the problem was that dull men often had no interest in such women and fell for people like Mma. Ramotswe. That was the trouble with people in general: they were surprisingly unrealistic in their expectations. Mma. Ramotswe smiled at the thought, remembering how, as a young woman, she had had a very tall friend who had been loved by an extremely short man. The short man looked up at the face of his beloved, from almost below her waist, and she looked down at him, almost squinting over the distance that separated them. That distance could have been one thousand miles or more—the breadth of the Kalahari and back; but the short man was not to realise that, and was to desist, heartsore, only when the tall girl's equally tall brother stooped down to look into his eyes and told him that he was no longer to look at his sister, even from a distance, or he would face some dire, unex-pressed consequence. Mma. Ramotswe felt sorry for the short man, of course, as she could never find it in herself to dismiss the feelings of others; he should have realised how impossible were his ambitions, but people never did.

Mr. J.L.B. Matekoni was a very good man, but, unlike Hector Mapondise, he could not be described as dull. That was not to say that he was exciting, in the way in which Note had seemed exciting; he was just easy company. You could sit with Mr. J.L.B. Matekoni for hours, during which he might say nothing very important, but what he said was never tedious. Certainly he talked about cars a great deal, as most men did, but what he had to say about them was very much more interesting than what other men had to say on the subject. Mr. J.L.B. Matekoni regarded cars as having personalities, and he could tell just by looking at a car what sort of owner it had.

"Cars speak about people," he had once explained to her. "They tell you everything you need to know."

It had struck Mma. Ramotswe as a strange thing to say, but Mr. J.L.B. Matekoni had gone on to illustrate his point with a number of telling examples. Had she ever seen the inside of the car belonging to Mr. Motobedi Palati, for example? He was an untidy man, whose tie was never straight and whose shirt was permanently hanging out of his trousers. Not surprisingly, the inside of his car was a mess, with unattached wires sticking out from under the dashboard and a hole underneath the driver's seat—so that dust swirled up into the car and covered everything with a brown layer. Or what about that rather intimidating nurs-ing sister from the Princess Marina Hospital, the one who had humiliated a well-known politician when she had heckled him at a public meeting, raising questions about nurses' pay that he sim-ply could not answer? Her car, as one might expect, was in pristine condition and smelled vaguely of antiseptic. He could come up with further examples if she wished, but the point was made, and Mma. Ramotswe nodded her head in understanding.

It was Mma. Ramotswe's tiny white van that had brought them together. Even before she had taken it for repair at Tlokweng Road Speedy Motors, she had been aware of Mr. J.L.B. Matekoni, as a rather quiet man who lived by himself in a house near the old Botswana Defence Force Club. She had wondered why he was by himself, which was so unusual in Botswana, but had not thought much about him until he had engaged her in conversation after he had serviced the van one day, and had warned her about the state of her tyres. Thereafter she had taken to dropping in to see him in the garage from time to time, exchanging views about the day's events and enjoying the tea which he brewed on an old stove in the corner of his office.

Then there had come that extraordinary day when the tiny white van had choked and refused to start, and he had spent an entire afternoon in the yard at Zebra Drive, the van's engine laid out in what seemed like a hundred pieces, its very heart exposed. He had put everything together and had come into the house as evening fell and they had sat together on her verandah. He had asked her to marry him, and she had said that she would, almost without thinking about it, because she realised that here was a man who was as good as her father, and that they would be happy together.

Mma. Ramotswe had not been prepared for Mr. J.L.B. Matekoni to fall ill, or at least to fall ill in the way in which he had done. It would have been easier, perhaps, if his illness had been one of the body, but it was his mind which was affected, and it seemed to her that the man she had known had simply vacated his body and gone somewhere else. Thanks to Mma. Silvia Potokwani, matron of the orphan farm, and to the drugs which Dr. Moffat gave to Mma. Potokwani to administer to Mr. J.L.B. Matekoni, the familiar personality returned. The obsessive brooding, the air of defeat, the lassitude—all these faded away and Mr. J.L.B. Matekoni began to smile again and take an interest in the business he had so uncharacteristically neglected.

Of course, during his illness he had been unable to run the garage, and it had been Mma. Ramotswe's assistant, Mma. Makutsi, who had managed to keep that going. Mma. Makutsi had done wonders with the garage. Not only had she made major steps in reforming the lazy apprentices, who had given Mr. J.L.B. Matekoni such trouble with their inconsiderate way with cars (one had even been seen to use a hammer on an engine), but she had attracted a great deal of new customers to the garage. An increasing number of women had their own cars now, and they were delighted to take them to a garage run by a lady. Mma. Makutsi may not have known a great deal about engines when she first started to run the garage, but she had learned quickly and was now quite capable of carrying out service and routine repairs on most makes of car, provided that they were not too modern and too dependent on temperamental devices of the sort which German car manufacturers liked to hide in cars to confuse mechanics elsewhere.

"What are we going to do to thank her?" asked Mma. Ramotswe. "She's put so much work into the garage, and now here you are back again, and she is just going to be an assistant manager and assistant private detective once more. It will be hard for her."

Mr. J.L.B. Matekoni frowned. "I would not like to upset her," he said. "You are right about how hard she has worked. I can see it in the books. Everything is in order. All the bills are paid, all the invoices properly numbered. Even the garage floor is cleaner, and there is less grease all over the place."

"And yet her life is not all that good," mused Mma. Ramotswe.

"She is living in that one room over at Old Naledi with a sick brother. I cannot pay her very much. And she has no husband to look after her. She deserves better than that."

Mr. J.L.B. Matekoni agreed. He would be able to help her by allowing her to continue as assistant manager of Tlokweng Road Speedy Motors, but it was difficult to see what he could do beyond that. Certainly the question of husbands had nothing to do with him. He was a man, after all, and the problems which single girls had in their lives were beyond him. It was women's business, he thought, to help their friends when it came to meeting people. Surely Mma. Ramotswe could advise her on the best tactics to adopt in that regard? Mma. Ramotswe was a popular woman who had many friends and admirers. Was there not something that Mma. Makutsi could do to find a husband? Surely she could be told how to go about it?

Mma. Ramotswe was not at all sure about this. "You have to be careful what you say," she warned Mr. J.L.B. Matekoni. "People don't like you to think that they know nothing. Especially somebody like Mma. Makutsi, with her ninety-seven percent or whatever it was. You can't go and tell somebody like that that they don't know a basic thing, such as how to find a husband."

"It's nothing to do with ninety-seven percent," said Mr. J.L.B. Matekoni. "You could get one hundred percent for typing and still not know how to talk to men. Getting married is different from being able to type. Quite different."

The mention of marriage had made Mma. Ramotswe wonder about when they were going to get married themselves, and she almost asked him about this but stopped. Dr. Moffat had explained to her that it was important that Mr. J.L.B. Matekoni should not be subjected to too much stress, even if he had recovered from the worst of his depression. It would undoubtedly be stressful for him if she started to ask about wedding dates, and so she said nothing about that and even agreed—for the sake of avoiding stress—to speak to Mma. Makutsi at some time in the near future with a view to finding out whether the issue of husbands could be helped in any way with a few well-chosen words of advice.

DURING MR. J.L.B. Matekoni's illness they had moved the No. 1 Ladies' Detective Agency into the back office at Tlokweng Road Speedy Motors. It had proved to be a successful arrangement: the affairs of the garage could be easily supervised from the back of the building, and there was a separate entrance for agency clients. Each business benefited in other ways. Those who brought their cars in for repair sometimes realised that there was a matter which might benefit from investigation—an errant husband, for example, or a missing relative—while others who came with a matter for the agency would arrange at the same time for their cars to be serviced or their brakes to be checked.

Mma. Ramotswe and Mma. Makutsi had arranged their desks in such a way that they could engage in conversation if they wished, without staring at one another all the time. If Mma. Ramotswe turned in her chair, she could address Mma. Makutsi on the other side of the room without having to twist her neck or talk over her shoulder, and Mma. Makutsi could do the same if she needed to ask Mma. Ramotswe for anything.

Now, with the day's post of four letters attended to and filed, Mma. Ramotswe suggested to her assistant that it was time for a cup of bush tea. This was a little earlier than normal, but it was a warm day and she always found that the best way of dealing with the heat was a cup of tea, accompanied by an Ouma's rusk dipped into the liquid until it was soft enough to be eaten without hurting the teeth.

"Mma. Makutsi," Mma. Ramotswe began after her assistant had delivered the cup of freshly made tea to her desk, "are you happy?"

Mma. Makutsi, who was halfway back to her desk, stopped where she stood. "Why do you ask, Mma.?" she said. "Why do you ask me if I'm happy?" The question had stopped her heart, as she lived in fear of losing her job and this question, she thought, could only be a preliminary to suggesting that she move on to another job. But there would be no other job, or at least no other job remotely like this one. Here she was an assistant detective and previously, possibly still, an acting garage manager. If she had to go somewhere else, then she would revert to being a junior clerk, at best, or a junior secretary at somebody else's beck and call. And she would never be as well paid as she was here, with the extra money that came to her for her garage work.

"Why don't you sit down, Mma.?" went on Mma. Ramotswe. "Then we can drink our tea together and you can tell me if you are happy."

Mma. Makutsi made her way back to her desk. She picked up her cup, but her hand shook and she put it down again. Why was life so unfair? Why did all the best jobs go to the beautiful girls, even if they barely got fifty percent in the examinations at the Botswana Secretarial College while she, with her results, had experienced such difficulty in finding a job at all? There was no obvious answer to that question. Unfairness seemed to be an inescapable feature of life, at least if you were Mma. Makutsi from Bobonong in northern Botswana, daughter of a man whose cattle had always been thin. Everything, it seemed, was unfair.

"I am very happy," said Mma. Makutsi miserably. "I am happy with this job. I do not want to go anywhere else."

Mma. Ramotswe laughed. "Oh, the job. Of course you're happy with that. We know that. And we're very happy with you.

Mr. J.L.B. Matekoni and I are very happy. You are our right-hand woman. Everybody knows that."

It took Mma. Makutsi a few moments to absorb this compliment, but when she did, she felt relief flood through her. She picked up her teacup, with a steady hand now, and took a deep draught of the hot red liquid.

"What I'm really wanting to find out," went on Mma. Ramotswe, "is whether you're happy in your . . . in yourself. Are you getting what you want out of life?"

Mma. Makutsi thought for a moment. "I'm not sure what I want out of life," she said after a while. "I used to think that I would like to be rich, but now that I've met some rich people I'm not so sure about that."

"Rich people are just people," said Mma. Ramotswe. "I have not met a rich person yet who isn't just the same as us. Being happy or unhappy has nothing to do with being rich."

Mma. Makutsi nodded. "So now I think that happiness comes from somewhere else. It comes from somewhere inside."

"Somewhere inside?"

Mma. Makutsi adjusted her large spectacles. She was an avid reader and enjoyed a serious conversation of this sort, in which she would be able to bring up snippets that she had garnered from old issues of the *National Geographic* or the *Mail and Guardian*.

"Happiness is found in the head," she said, warming to the subject. "If the head is full of happiness, then the person is definitely happy. That is clearly true."

"And the heart?" ventured Mma. Ramotswe. "Does the heart not come into it?"

There was a silence. Mma. Makutsi looked down, tracing a pattern with her finger on a dusty corner of her desktop. "The heart is the place where love happens," she said quietly.

Mma. Ramotswe took a deep breath. "Would you not like to

have a husband, Mma. Makutsi?" she said gently. "Would it not make you happier to have a husband to look after you?" She paused and then added, "I was just wondering, that's all."

Mma. Makutsi looked at her. Then she took off her glasses and polished them with a corner of her handkerchief. It was a favourite handkerchief of hers—with lace at the edges—but now it was threadbare from so much use and could not last much longer. But she loved it still and would buy another one just like it when she had the money.

"I would like to have a husband," she said. "But there are many beautiful girls. They are the ones who are getting the husbands. There is nobody left over for me."

"But you are a very good-looking lady," said Mma. Ramotswe stoutly. "I am sure that there are many men who will agree with me."

Mma. Makutsi shook her head. "I do not think so, Mma.," she said. "Although you are very kind to say that to me."

"Perhaps you should try to find a man," said Mma. Ramotswe. "Maybe you should be doing a bit more about it if no men are coming your way. Try to find them."

"Where?" asked Mma. Makutsi. "Where are these men you are talking about?"

Mma. Ramotswe waved a hand in the direction of the door, and of Africa outside. "Out there," she said. "There are men out there. You have to meet them."

"Where exactly?" asked Mma. Makutsi.

"In the middle of the town," said Mma. Ramotswe. "You see them sitting about at lunchtime. Men. Plenty of them."

"All married," said Mma. Makutsi.

"Or in bars," said Mma. Ramotswe, feeling that the conversation was not taking the turn she had planned for it.

"But you know what they are like in bars," said Mma. Makutsi. "Bars are full of men who are looking for bad girls."

Mma. Ramotswe had to agree. Bars were full of men like Note Mokoti and his friends, and she would never wish anybody like that on Mma. Makutsi. It would be far better to be single than to become involved with somebody who would only make you unhappy.

"It is kind of you to think of me like this," said Mma. Makutsi after a while. "But you and Mr. J.L.B. Matekoni mustn't worry about me. I am happy enough, and if there is going to be somebody for me, then I am sure that I shall meet him. Then everything will change."

Mma. Ramotswe grasped at the opportunity to bring the conversation to an end. "I'm sure that you are right," she said.

"Perhaps," said Mma. Makutsi.

Mma. Ramotswe busied herself with a sheaf of papers on her desk. She felt saddened by the air of defeat which seemed to descend upon her assistant whenever the conversation turned to her personal circumstances. There was no real need for Mma. Makutsi to feel like this. She might have had difficulties in her life until now—certainly one should not underestimate what it must be like to grow up in Bobonong, that rather dry and distant place from where Mma. Makutsi had come—but there were plenty of people who came from places like that and made something of their lives in spite of their origins. If you went through life thinking, *I'm just a local girl from somewhere out in the bush,* then what was the point of making any effort? We all had to come from somewhere, and most of us came from somewhere not particularly impressive. Even if you were born in Gaborone, you had to come from a particular house in Gaborone, and ultimately that meant that you came from just a small patch of the earth; and that was no different from any other patch of the earth anywhere else.

Mma. Makutsi should make more of herself, thought Mma. Ramotswe. She should remember who she was—which was a citizen of Botswana, of the finest country in Africa, and one of the most distinguished graduates of the Botswana Secretarial College. Both of those were matters of which one could be justly proud. You could be proud to be a Motswana, because your country had never done anything of which to feel ashamed. It had conducted itself with complete integrity, even in times when it had to contend with neighbours in a state of civil war. It had always been honest, too, without that ruinous corruption that had shamed so many other countries in Africa, and which had bled away the wealth of an entire continent. They had never stooped to that, because Sir Seretse Khama, that great man whom her father had once greeted personally at Mochudi, had made it clear to every single citizen that there was to be no taking or giving of bribes, no dipping into money that belonged to the country. And everyone had listened to him and obeyed this precept because they could recognise in him the qualities of chiefly greatness which his forebears, the Khamas, had always possessed. Those qualities could not be acquired overnight, but they took generations to mature (whatever people said). That was why when Queen Elizabeth II met Seretse Khama, she knew immediately what sort of man he was. She knew because she could tell that he was the same sort of person as she was: a person who had been brought up to serve. Mma. Ramotswe knew all this, but she sometimes wondered whether people who were slightly younger—people like Mma. Makutsi—were aware of what a great man the first president of Botswana had been and of how he had been admired by the queen herself. Or would it mean anything to her? Would she *understand?*

Mma. Ramotswe was a royalist, of course. She admired monarchs, as long as they were respectable and behaved in the correct way. She admired the king of Lesotho, because he was a direct descendant of Moshoeshoe I, who had saved his country from the Boers and who had been a good, wise man (and modest, too—had he not described himself as the flea in the blanket of Queen Victoria?). She admired the old king of Swaziland, King Sobhuza II, who had had one hundred and forty-one wives, all at the same time. She admired him in spite of his having all those wives, which, after all, was a very traditional approach to life; she admired him because he loved his people and because he consistently refused to allow the death penalty to be exacted, always— with only one exception in his long reign, a most serious case of witchcraft murder—granting mercy at the last moment. (What sort of man, she wondered, could coldly say to another who was begging for his life: *no, you must die?*) There were other kings and queens, of course, not just African ones. There was the late queen of Tonga, who was a very special queen, because she was so fat. Mma. Ramotswe had seen a picture of her in an encyclopaedia, and it had covered two pages, so wide was the queen. And there was the Dutch queen, of whom she had seen a photograph in a magazine, enigmatically described in the caption below the picture as the Orange Queen. And indeed she had been wearing a dark orange outfit and two-tone orange and brown shoes. Mma. Ramotswe thought that she might like to meet that queen, who looked so cheerful and smiled so warmly (and what, she wondered, was this House of Orange in which this queen was said to live?). Maybe she would come to Botswana one day, in her two-tone shoes perhaps; but one should not hope too much. Nobody came to Botswana, because people just did not know about it. They had not heard. They just had not heard.

Mma. Makutsi might do well to reflect on the example of this Orange Queen, with her pleasant smile and self-evidently optimistic outlook. She should remind herself that even if she did come from Bobonong, she had put that behind her and was now a person who lived in the capital, in Gaborone itself. She should also remind herself that even if she thought that her complexion was too dark, there were plenty of men who were very happy with women who looked that way rather than those pallid creatures one sometimes saw who had made their skins look blotchy with lightening creams. And as for those large glasses which Mma. Makutsi wore, there might be some who would find them a little bit intimidating, but many other men simply would fail to notice them, in much the same way as they failed to notice what women were wearing in general, no matter what efforts women made with their clothing.

The trouble with men, of course, was that they went about with their eyes half closed for much of the time. Sometimes Mma. Ramotswe wondered whether men actually wanted to see anything, or whether they decided that they would notice only the things that interested them. That was why women were so good at tasks which required attention to the way people felt. Being a private detective, for example, was exactly the sort of job at which a woman could be expected to excel (and look at the success of the No. 1 Ladies' Detective Agency). That was because women watched and tried to understand what was going on in people's minds. Of course there were some men who could do this—one thought immediately of Clovis Andersen, author of *The Principles of Private Detection,* Mma. Ramotswe's well-thumbed copy of which occupied pride of place on the shelf behind her desk. Clovis Andersen must be a most sympathetic man, Mma. Ramotswe thought; more like a woman, in many ways, with his advice to study people's clothing carefully. *(There are many clues in what people wear, he wrote. Our clothes reveal a great deal about us. They talk. A man who wears no tie does not dress that way because he has no tie—he probably has an appreciable number of ties in his wardrobe at home—he is wearing no tie because he has chosen to do so. That means that he wishes to appear casual.)* Mma.

Ramotswe had found that a puzzling passage and had wondered where it was leading. She was not sure what one could deduce from the fact that a man wished to appear casual, but she was sure that, like all the observations of Clovis Andersen, this was in some way important.

She looked up from her desk and glanced at Mma. Makutsi, who was busying herself with the typing of a letter which Mma. Ramotswe had drafted, in pencil, earlier on. *We must try to help her,* she thought. *We must try to persuade her to value herself more than she does at present.* She was a fine woman, with great talents, and it was absurd that she should go through life thinking less of herself because she had no husband. That was such a waste. Mma. Makutsi deserved to be happy. She deserved to have something to look forward to other than a bleak existence in one room in Old Naledi; a room that she shared with her sick brother, and into which no light came. Everybody deserved more than that, even in this unlucky world, a world which had brought such rewards to Mma. Ramotswe but which seemed to be grudging in its appreciation of Mma. Makutsi. *We shall change all that,* thought Mma. Ramotswe, *because it is possible to change the world, if one is determined enough, and if one sees with sufficient clarity just what it is that has to be changed.*

()

CHAPTER TWO

LEARN TO DRIVE WITH JESUS

LIFE AT Tlokweng Road Speedy Motors (and, indeed, at the No. 1
Ladies' Detective Agency) was returning to normal. Mr. J.L.B.
Matekoni had resumed his old practice of coming in to work
shortly before seven in the morning, and would already be pros-
trate on his inspection board shining a torch up into a car's under-
belly by the time the two apprentices arrived at eight o'clock.
Their contract of apprenticeship stipulated that they should work
eight hours a day, with time off for study every three months, but
Mr. J.L.B. Matekoni had given up expecting them to comply with
this. Certainly they arrived at eight and left at five, which made
nine hours each day, but from this total there was deducted an
hour for lunch, and two tea-breaks of forty-five minutes each. It
was the tea-breaks that were the problem, but any attempt to
insist on a far shorter break had been met with sullen resistance.
Eventually he had given up; he was a generous man and did not
like conflict.

"You may have it easy here," he had warned them on more than
one occasion, "but don't think that all bosses are like this. When
you finish your apprenticeship—*if you finish*—then you'll have to
find another job, a real job, and you'll learn all about it then."

"Learn about what, boss?" asked the older apprentice, smiling conspiratorially at his friend.

"About the working world," said Mr. J.L.B. Matekoni. "About what it's like to be kept really hard at it."

The older apprentice rolled his eyes in mock horror. "But you'll keep us on here, won't you, boss? You couldn't do without us, could you?"

The arrival of Mma. Makutsi as acting manager of the garage had brought about a change, even if the long tea-breaks survived. She had quickly shown that she would take no nonsense from the two apprentices, and they had rapidly abandoned their slovenly ways. Mma. Ramotswe had been unable to work out what lay behind the change, so dramatic was it; she had assumed that it was something to do with working for a woman, which may have encouraged them to show what they could do, but she had eventually thought that it was something deeper than that. Certainly the two boys had wanted to impress her, but it seemed, too, that she had instilled in them a real pride in their work. Now, with Mr. J.L.B. Matekoni back in the garage, both Mma. Ramotswe and Mma. Makutsi were anxious to see whether the change would prove to be permanent.

"Those two boys are much better," remarked Mr. J.L.B. Matekoni shortly after his return. "They're still a bit lazy, which is probably just their nature, and they still talk endlessly about girls, which may also be their nature, come to think of it. But I think that their work is much neater . . . much less . . . less. . . ."

"Greasy?" prompted Mma. Ramotswe.

"Yes," agreed Mr. J.L.B. Matekoni. "That's it. They used to be so messy, as you know, but now that's all changed. And they're also not so brutal with the engines. They seemed to have learned something while I was away."

And there were further changes—changes of which Mr.

J.L.B. Matekoni as yet had no inkling. It was Mma. Ramotswe, in fact, who first became aware that something had happened, and she sought confirmation from Mma. Makutsi before she made any remark to Mr. J.L.B. Matekoni. Mma. Makutsi was astonished; she had been too busy to have noticed, she remarked in her defence, otherwise she would surely have picked up something like that. Now, after she had spoken discreetly to Charlie, the elder of the two apprentices, she was able to confirm Mma. Ramotswe's suspicions.

"You're right," she said. "The younger one has heard about the Lord. And he was the one who was by far the worst with the girls—always going on about them, remember—and now there he is, joined up to one of those marching churches. The Lord told him to do it, Charlie said. He's surprised, too. He's very disappointed that he doesn't seem to be too keen to talk about girls anymore. Charlie doesn't like that."

The news was passed on to Mr. J.L.B. Matekoni, who sighed. These apprentices were a mystery to him, and he looked forward to the day when they would be off his hands, if that day were ever to come. Life had become much more complicated for him, and he was not sure whether he liked it that way. In the past it had been simple: he had been alone at the garage and had only himself to worry about. Now there were Mma. Makutsi, the two apprentices, and Mma. Ramotswe, and that was even before one took into account the two orphans whose fostering he had arranged. That had been a very rash act on his part, although it was not one which he really regretted. The children were so happy staying in Mma. Ramotswe's house on Zebra Drive that it would have been churlish beyond measure to begrudge them that. But, even then, to go from being responsible for one person, himself, to being responsible for six was a step which might daunt any man, no matter how broad his shoulders.

While Mr. J.L.B. Matekoni imagined that he was responsible for others, they imagined that they were responsible for him. Mma. Makutsi, for example, had taken her role within the garage with immense seriousness. She had changed the system of book-keeping and had improved the flow of cash; she had conducted a full inventory of stock and had listed all spare parts held in the storeroom, and she had sorted out the fuel receipts, which had been allowed to get into a terrible state. All of this was an achievement, she knew, but she was still worried. The No. 1 Ladies' Detective Agency did not make a large profit, even if it did at least make some money. The garage did better, but the apprentices' wages were a major drain on that side of the business. If they wanted to prosper, particularly when bank charges were going up, they would just have to find more business, or—and this she found an intriguing possibility—they would have to diversify. It had been a challenge to take on responsibility for a garage; why not take on something else as well? For a moment she felt quite dizzy, contemplating the possibility of a sprawling business. Fac-tories, farms, stores—all of these were possible if one only tried. But where would one start? The marriage of the No. 1 Ladies' Detective Agency to Tlokweng Road Speedy Motors had been a natural development, following on the engagement of the owners of the two concerns; finding something entirely new might be rather more difficult.

The idea came to Mma. Makutsi one morning when she was preparing a cup of bush tea. Mma. Ramotswe was out shopping and Mr. J.L.B. Matekoni had driven off to look at a car which he had offered to sell on behalf of an old client. It was not much of a car, he had told her, but he regarded himself as responsible for his clients' cars from birth to death, so to speak, as an old-fashioned doctor would see his patients through life's journey. She took the freshly brewed tea into the garage workshop, where the two apprentices were sitting on a couple of upturned oil drums, watching a thin stray dog nose about the entrance to the garage.

"You look very busy," said Mma. Makutsi.

The older apprentice looked up at her resentfully. "It's our tea-break, Mma. Same as yours. We can't work all the time."

Mma. Makutsi nodded. She was not interested in giving the apprentices one of the periodic dressings-down that had proved to be so effective while Mr. J.L.B. Matekoni was away; she wanted their reaction to her idea.

"I've thought of a new thing for the business to do," she announced, taking a sip of her bush tea. "I wondered what you would think."

"You are a lady who is full of ideas," said the younger apprentice. "Your head must hurt, Mma."

Mma. Makutsi smiled. "Only hard ideas make your head hurt. My ideas are always simple."

"I have simple ideas, too," said the older apprentice. "I have ideas of girls. Those are my ideas. Simple. Girls, and then more girls."

Mma. Makutsi ignored this, addressing her next remark to the younger apprentice. "There are many people wanting to learn how to drive, are there not?"

The younger apprentice shrugged. "They can learn. There are lots of bush roads for them to practise on."

"But that won't help them drive in town," said Mma. Makutsi quickly. "There are too many things happening in town. There are cars going this way and that. There are people crossing the road."

"And lots of girls," interjected the older apprentice. "Lots of girls walking about. All the time."

The younger apprentice turned to look at his friend. "What is wrong with you? You are always thinking of girls."

"So are you," snapped the other. "Anyone who says he does

not think of girls is a liar. All men think of girls. That is what men like to do."

"Not all the time," said the younger one. "There are other things to think about."

"That is not true," the older one retorted. "If you didn't think about girls, then it is a sign that you are about to die. That is a well-known fact."

"I am not interested in any of this," said Mma. Makutsi. "And, anyway, I'd heard that one of you has changed." She paused, looking at the younger one for confirmation; but he merely lowered his eyes.

"So," she continued, "I will tell you of an idea that I have had. I think that it is a good idea and I would like to hear what you think of it."

"You can tell us," said the older apprentice. "We are listening to what you have to say."

Mma. Makutsi dropped her voice, as if there were eavesdroppers in the darker corners of the garage. The apprentices leaned forward to catch her words. "I have decided that we should open a driving school," she announced. "I will make some enquiries, but I do not think that there are enough driving schools. We could start a new one and give people a lesson after work. We could charge forty pula a time. Twenty pula could go to the teacher and twenty pula to Mr. J.L.B. Matekoni for the garage and for using his car. It would be a great success."

The apprentices stared at her, and for a few moments nothing was said. Then the older one spoke.

"I do not want to have anything to do with it," he said. "After work I like to go to see my friends. I do not have time to take people for driving lessons."

Mma. Makutsi looked at his friend. "And you?"

The younger apprentice smiled back at her. "You are a very clever lady, Mma. I think that this is a good idea."

"There!" said Mma. Makutsi, turning to the older apprentice. "You see, your friend here has a more positive way of looking at things. You are just useless. Look what all that thinking about girls has done to your brain."

The younger apprentice smirked. "You hear that? Mma. Makutsi is right. You should listen to her." He turned to Mma. Makutsi. "What will you call this driving school, Mma.?"

"I have not thought about it," she said. "I will think of something. The name you give to a business is very important. That is why the No. 1 Ladies' Detective Agency has been a success. The name says everything you need to know about the business."

The younger apprentice looked up at her hopefully. "I have a good idea for the name," he said. "We could call it *Learn to Drive with Jesus.*"

There was a silence. The older apprentice cast a glance in the direction of his friend and then turned away.

"I am not sure about that," said Mma. Makutsi. "I will think about it, but I am not sure."

"It is a very good name," said the younger apprentice. "It will attract a careful class of driver, and it will mean that we have no accidents. The Lord will look after us.

"I hope so," said Mma. Makutsi. "I shall talk to Mr. J.L.B. Matekoni about it and see what he thinks. Thank you for the suggestion."

CHAPTER THREE

TO KILL A HOOPOE

MMA. RAMOTSWE completed her shopping. Before the two orphans had come to stay, shopping had been an easy task and she found that she rarely had to get supplies more than once a week. Now it seemed that everything ran out shortly after she had replenished stocks. Only two days ago she had bought flour—a large bag, too—and now the flour was finished and the cake baked by the girl, Motholeli, had been all but consumed by her brother, Puso. That was a good sign, of course: boys should have good appetites, and it was natural for them to want to eat large amounts of cake and sweet things. As they grew older, they would move to meat, which was very important for a man. But all this food that was being consumed cost money, and had it not been for the generous contributions made by Mr. J.L.B. Matekoni—contributions which in fact covered the entire cost of keeping the children—Mma. Ramotswe would have begun to feel the pinch.

It was Mr. J.L.B. Matekoni's idea to foster the children in the first place, and although she never regretted taking them in, she wished that he had consulted her first. It was not that she resented the fact that Motholeli was confined to a wheelchair and that she was now responsible for a handicapped child, it was just that she had imagined that something quite as important as this would have been the subject of some discussion. But it was not in Mr. J.L.B. Matekoni's heart to say no—that was the problem. And she loved him all the more for that. Mma. Silvia Potokwani, matron of the orphan farm, had understood that very well and, as usual, had been able to ensure the best possible arrangements for her orphans. She must have been planning for months to place the orphans with him, and of course she must have realised that they would end up living in Mma. Ramotswe's house in Zebra Drive rather than in Mr. J.L.B. Matekoni's house near the old Botswana Defence Club. Of course, after the marriage (whenever that would be), they would all live together under one roof. The children had already been asking about that, and she had told them that she was waiting for Mr. J.L.B. Matekoni to decide on a date.

"He does not rush things," she had explained. "Mr. J.L.B. Matekoni is a very careful man. He likes to do things slowly."

Puso had seemed impatient, and she had realised that his need was for a father. Mr. J.L.B. Matekoni would be that in due course, but in the meantime the boy, who had never had a parent, would be wondering whether he ever would. At the age of six, a week was a long time; a month would be interminable.

Motholeli, who had suffered so much and who had been so brave, understood. She had been used to waiting and of course it took her much longer to do anything, manoeuvring her wheelchair with difficulty through doorways that always seemed too small or along corridors that ended in awkward steps. Only now and then did she seem to register disappointment, and that was never for more than a few moments. So when Mma. Ramotswe returned from her shopping and struggled into the kitchen, laden with brown paper bags, she was surprised to find that there was no cheerful greeting from Motholeli, only a downcast look.

She lowered her parcels onto the table. "So much shopping,"

she said. "Lots of meat. A sort of chicken." She paused. She knew
that Motholeli liked pumpkins. "And a pumpkin," she said, adding:
"A big one. Very yellow."

At first the girl said nothing. Then, when she replied, her
voice was flat: "That is good."

Mma. Ramotswe looked at her. Motholeli had left that morning in good spirits, and so it must have been something which
had happened at school. She remembered her own school days
and the ups and downs which she had experienced. They had
been such little dramas—at least when looked at from her current perspective—but they had seemed so grave and frightening
at the time. She remembered the occasion when the head
teacher of her school at Mochudi had tried to flush out a thief.
One of the children had been stealing, and the teacher had sum-
moned every child into his office and had insisted that he or she
place a hand on the large Setswana Bible which he kept on his
table. Then each child had been asked to say, beneath the head
teacher's piercing gaze: *I swear that I am not a thief.*

"Nobody who is innocent has anything to fear," the teacher
had announced before the whole school, assembled on the dusty
playing field. "But the person who lies with his hand on the Bible
will be struck down. That is one thing that is sure. Maybe not
straightaway, but later, when you are not expecting it. That is
when the Lord will strike you down."

The silence had been complete. She had looked up into the
sky but had seen only utter emptiness. It was undoubtedly true,
of course; people were struck by lightning, and it must have been
because they deserved it: thieves, perhaps, or even worse. She
had no doubt but that the thief, whoever it was, would know this
just as she did and would falter before he uttered the fateful
words. But when the last pupil had filed out of the office and the
head teacher had come out looking angry, she realised that she

had been wrong and that one of their number was now in mortal danger. Who could it be? She had her suspicions, of course; everybody knew that Elijah Sebekedi could not be trusted, and although nobody had actually seen him stealing anything, how could he afford to buy those tins of condensed milk which he drank so conspicuously on his way home from school? His father, as was well known, was a drunkard and spent all his money on traditional beer, leaving nothing for his family. The children survived on handouts; the shoes they wore, the clothes, were recognised by the other children as those which they had abandoned, thinking that no more wear could be extracted from them. So there was only one explanation for Elijah's tins of condensed milk.

She thought about him that night as she lay on her sleeping mat, watching the square of moonlight move slowly across the wall opposite her bedroom window. The rainy season was not far away, and there would be storms. Elijah Sebekedi should be worried about that; there would be lightning about. She closed her eyes, and then, her heart pounding, she opened them again. She herself had lied! Only a week ago she had helped herself to a doughnut which she had found in the kitchen. She had been unable to resist it and had felt immediately guilty after she had finished licking the last of the sugar off her fingers. She had said *I swear that I am not a thief,* blatantly, falsely, and had repeated it as the head teacher had not heard her the first time that she had uttered those fateful, damning words. And now she would be struck by lightning; there was no escape.

SHE DID not sleep well, and the next morning she was silent as she ate her breakfast in the kitchen. Mma. Ramotswe had lost her mother when she was still young and was looked after by her father and several of his female relatives who took it in turns to keep house for them. There was a seemingly endless supply of these relatives—competent, cheerful women who appeared to look forward to their turn to come to Mochudi and to rearrange and reverse everything which their predecessor had done in the house. These were house-proud women, who kept the yard spotless, the sand brushed and raked every day, the chicken manure cleared away and deposited on the melon patch; women who understood the importance of scouring your pans until the black was scraped away and the metal below was shining. These were not small things. These were the things which showed children growing up in the house how they should live their lives as clean, upright people.

Now, sitting at the kitchen table with her father and his aunt from Palapye, watching the soft rays of the early morning sun streaming in through the door, Precious Ramotswe was aware that if it clouded over—as it might—and if there were lightning—as there might be—then she might not be sitting here the next morning. Of course there was only one thing to do, which was to confess, which she did, there and then to her father and the aunt, and Obed Ramotswe, after listening to her with astonishment, had turned to his aunt, and she had laughed and said: "But that was meant for you, that doughnut. You did not steal it." And at this, overcome with relief, Precious had burst into tears and told the adults of the fate that awaited Elijah. Obed Ramotswe exchanged glances with his aunt.

"That is a very unkind thing to do to children," he said. "That poor boy will not be struck by lightning. Maybe he will learn one day not to be a thief. It is for his father to teach him that, but he is always drinking." He paused. It was a grave thing to criticise a teacher, especially in front of a child, but the words came out before he could stop them: "The Lord is more likely to strike the head teacher than that boy."

Mma. Ramotswe had not thought of this incident for years, and now, looking at Motholeli, she wondered what local torment was causing her unhappiness. People said that school days were happy, but they often were not. Often it was like being in prison; wary of older children and terrified of teachers, unable to talk to anybody about troubles because you thought that there would be nobody who would understand. Perhaps things had changed for the better, and in some ways they had. Teachers were not allowed to beat children as they did in the past, although, Mma. Ramotswe reflected, there were some boys—and indeed some young men—who might have been greatly improved by moderate physical correction. The apprentices, for example: would it help if Mr. J.L.B. Matekoni resorted to physical chastisement—nothing severe, of course—but just an occasional kick in the seat of the pants while they were bending over to change a tyre or something like that? The thought made her smile. She would even offer to administer the kick herself, which she imagined might be oddly satisfying, as one of the apprentices, the one who still kept on about girls, had a largeish bottom which she thought would be quite comfortable to kick. How enjoyable it would be to creep up behind him and kick him when he was least expecting it, and then to say: *Let that be a lesson!* That was all one would have to say, but it would be a blow for women everywhere.

But those were not serious thoughts and would not help the immediate problem, which was to find out what was troubling Motholeli and making her so palpably miserable.

Mma. Ramotswe put away the last of her groceries and then put on the kettle to make a pot of red bush tea. Then she sat down.

"You're unhappy," she said simply. "And it's something at school, isn't it?"

Motholeli shook her head. "No," she said. "I am not."

"That is not true," said Mma. Ramotswe. "You are a happy girl normally. You are famous for your happiness. And now you are almost crying. I do not have to be a detective to know that."

The girl looked down at the ground.

"I have no mother," she said quietly. "I am a girl who has no mother."

Something caught at Mma. Ramotswe's throat: a feeling of sudden, overwhelming sympathy. So that was it. She was missing her mother; of course she was. She was missing her mother in exactly the same way in which she, Precious Ramotswe, had missed her own mother, whom she had never known, and in the same way, too, that she missed her father, every day of her life, every day, her good, kind father, Obed Ramotswe, of whom she was so proud. Mma. Ramotswe rose to her feet and crossed the kitchen floor. Now she crouched down and embraced the girl.

"Of course you have a mother, Motholeli," she whispered. "Your mummy is there, in heaven, and she is watching you, watching you every day. And I'll tell you what she's thinking: she's thinking, *I am very proud of that fine girl, my daughter. I am very proud of how hard she is working and how she is looking after her little brother.* That is what she is thinking."

She felt the girl's shoulder heave beneath her and she felt the warm tears of the child against her own skin.

"You mustn't cry," she said. "You mustn't be unhappy. She would not want you to be unhappy, would she?"

"She doesn't care. She doesn't care what happens to me."

Mma. Ramotswe caught her breath. "But you mustn't say that. That is not true. It is not. Of course she cares."

"That is not what this girl is telling me at school," said Motholeli. "She says that I am a girl who has no mother because my mother did not like me and left. That is what she says."

"And who is this girl?" asked Mma. Ramotswe angrily. "Who is she to tell you these lies?"

"She is a very popular girl at school. She is a rich girl. She has many friends, and they all believe what she says."

"Her name?" said Mma. Ramotswe. "What is the name of this popular girl?"

Motholeli gave the name, and Mma. Ramotswe immediately knew. For a moment she said nothing, then, wiping the tears away from Motholeli's cheek, she spoke to her.

"We will talk about this more later on," she said. "For now, you just remember that everything that this girl has said to you—everything—is just not true. It doesn't matter who she is. It doesn't matter one little bit. You lost your mother because she was sick. She was a good woman, I know that. I have asked about her, and that is what Mma. Potokwani told me. She said she was a strong woman who was kind to people. You remember that. You remember that and be proud of it. Do you understand what I am saying?"

The girl looked up. Then she nodded.

"And there is something else you must remember," Mma. Ramotswe said. "There is something else that you must remember for the rest of your life. Sir Seretse Khama said that every person in Botswana, every person, is of equal value. The same. That means you, too. Everyone. You may be an orphan girl, but you are as good as anybody else. There is nobody who can look at you and say, *I am better than you*. Do you understand that?"

Mma. Ramotswe waited until Motholeli had nodded before she rose to her feet. "And in the meantime," she said, "we should start cooking this fine pumpkin so that when Mr. J.L.B. Matekoni comes to have dinner with us this evening, we shall have a good meal ready for him on the table. Would you like that?"

Motholeli smiled. "I would like that very much, Mma."

"Good," said Mma. Ramotswe.

MR. J.L.B. Matekoni left the garage at five o'clock and drove straight to the house in Zebra Drive. He liked the early evening, when the heat had gone out of the sun and it was pleasant to walk about in the last hour or so before dusk set in. This evening he was planning to spend some time clearing Mma. Ramotswe's vegetable garden at the back of the house before he would join her for a cup of bush tea on the verandah. There they would catch up on the day's events before going in for dinner. There was always something to discuss; information which Mma. Ramotswe had picked up while doing her shopping or items from that day's *Botswana Daily News* (except for football news, in which Mma. Ramotswe had no interest). They always agreed with one another; Mr. J.L.B. Matekoni trusted Mma. Ramotswe's judgement on matters of human nature and local politics, while she deferred to him on business issues and agriculture. Was the price of cattle too low at the moment, or was it reasonable enough, given the price that the canning factory and the butchers were prepared to pay? Mr. J.L.B. Matekoni would know the answer to that, and in Mma. Ramotswe's experience he was always right on these issues. What about that new politician, the one who had just been made a junior minister; was he to be trusted, or was he interested only in himself or, at a pinch, in the welfare of his own people in the town he came from? Only in himself, Mma. Ramotswe would say without hesitation; look at him, just look at the way that he holds his hands clasped in front of him when he talks. That's always a sign; always.

Mr. J.L.B. Matekoni parked his car just inside the gate. He liked to leave it there, allowing ample room for Mma. Ramotswe to drive past in her tiny white van, if she needed to go out. Then, changing from his garage shoes, which were always covered in oil, to the scuffed and dusty suede veldschoens that he liked to wear outside, Mr. J.L.B. Matekoni made his way to the back of the yard where he had planted several rows of beans under an awning of shade netting. In a dry country like Botswana, shade netting made all the difference to a plant's chances, keeping the drying rays of the sun off the vulnerable green leaves and allowing the earth to retain a little of any precious moisture left over from watering. The ground was always so thirsty; water poured upon it was soaked up with a parched eagerness that left little trace. But people persisted in spite of this and tried to make small patches of green amid the brown.

The yard in Zebra Drive was considerably larger than neighbouring plots. Mma. Ramotswe had always intended to clear it entirely but had never got round to cutting back the tangle of bush—stunted thorn trees, high grass, and sundry shrubs—which overgrew the back section of her plot. Behind it was a small stretch of wasteland, also overgrown, across which an informal path wound its way. People liked to use this as a shortcut to town, and in the morning one might hear whistling or singing from men on bicycles as they rode along the path. Babies were conceived here, too, especially on Saturday evenings, and Mma. Ramotswe had often thought that at least some of the children whom she saw playing games there had been drawn back by some strange homing instinct to revisit the place where they had started out.

Mr. J.L.B. Matekoni filled an old watering can from the standpipe at the side of the house. Inside the kitchen, Mma. Ramotswe heard the rap running and looked out of the window. She waved to her fiancé, who waved back, mouthing a few words of greeting to her, before he carried the can off to the vegetable plot. Mma. Ramotswe smiled to herself, and thought, *Here I am at last, with a good man, who is prepared to work in the garden and grow beans for me.* It was a comforting thought, and it made her feel warm with pleasure as she watched his retreating form disappear behind the clump of acacias that masked the rear portion of the yard.

Mr. J.L.B. Matekoni stooped under the shade netting and began to pour water, gently, almost dribbling it, against the lower stem of each bean plant. Every drop of water was precious in Botswana, and one would have to be foolhardy to use a hose to splash water all over the place. It was even more effective, if one had the resources, to set up a drip feed system, in which the water would travel down from a central reservoir on a thin line of cotton thread which would dip down into the ground at the plant's roots. That was the best water husbandry of all: tiny trickles of water delivered to the roots, minuscule drop by minuscule drop. *Perhaps one day I shall do that,* thought Mr. J.L.B. Matekoni. *Perhaps I shall do that when I am too old to fix cars anymore and have sold Tlokweng Road Speedy Motors. Then I shall be a farmer, as all my people have been before me. I shall go back to my lands, way out there on the edge of the Kalahari, and sit under a tree and watch my melons grow in the sun.*

He bent down to examine one of the bean plants, which had become entangled in the string up which it grew. As he gently redirected the plant's stem, there was a sudden noise behind him; a little thud, as of a stone hitting something, and then a dry, scrabbling noise, and he spun round immediately. A noise like that could easily be a snake; one had to be constantly on the watch for snakes, which might be lying anywhere and might suddenly rear up and strike. A cobra would be bad enough—and he had experienced several rather too close encounters with them— but what if it was a mamba, angered by a disturbance? Mambas were aggressive snakes which did not like people treading on their ground, and which would attack with real anger. A bite from a mamba was rarely survivable, as their poison travelled so quickly through the body and paralysed the lungs and the heart.

It was not a snake but a bird, which had fluttered down from the bough of a tree and had flown, at a strange angle, down against the shade netting. Now it had fallen to the ground and was beating its wings against the sand, raising a small cloud of dust. After a few struggling movements, it lay still, a hoopoe, with its gorgeous striped plumage and its tiny crown of black and white feathers sticking up like the headdress of some miniature chieftain.

Mr. J.L.B. Matekoni reached down to the bird, which watched his approaching hand with a liquid stare, but which seemed unable to move any longer. Its breast rose under the feathers, almost imperceptibly, and then was still. He picked it up still warm but now limp, and he turned it over. On its other side, the tiny eye—a black speck like the pip of a papaw—was hanging out of its socket, and there was a red patch in the plumage where the bird had been struck by a stone.

"Oh," said Mr. J.L.B. Matekoni, and then again, "Oh."

He laid the bird down on the ground and looked about him, out into the scrub bush.

"You skellums," he shouted. "I saw this! I saw you kill this bird!"

Boys, he thought. It would be boys with their catapults, hiding in the bushes and killing birds, not to eat, of course, but just killing them. Killing doves or pigeons was one thing; they could be eaten, but nobody could eat a hoopoe, and who could possibly wish to kill such a friendly little bird? You simply did not kill hoopoes.

Of course it would be impossible to catch the boys in question; they would have run away by now, or they would be hiding in the bush laughing at him behind their hands. There was nothing to be done but to toss the little carcass away. Rats would find it, or maybe a snake, and make a meal of it. This little death would be a windfall for somebody.

WHEN MR. J.L.B. Matekoni went back to the house, discouraged by the hoopoe's death, and by the condition of the beans, and by everything, he found Mma. Ramotswe waiting for him at the kitchen door.

"Have you seen Puso?" she asked. "He was playing out in the yard. But now it is dinnertime and he has not come back. You may have heard me calling him."

"I have not seen him," said Mr. J.L.B. Matekoni. "I have been out at the back . . ." He stopped.

"And?" said Mma. Ramotswe. "Is he back there?"

Mr. J.L.B. Matekoni hesitated for a moment.

"I think he is," he said gravely. "I think he is using a catapult out there."

They both went out to the vegetable patch and peered into the bush on the other side of the fence.

"Puso," called out Mma. Ramotswe. "We know that you are hiding. You come out or I shall come and get you myself.

They waited for a few moments. Then Mma. Ramotswe called out again.

"Puso! You are there! We know you are there!"

Mr. J.L.B. Matekoni thought he saw a movement in the high grass. It was a good place for a boy to hide, but it would be easy enough to go and get him out if they had to.

"Puso!" shouted Mma. Ramotswe. "You are there! Come out!"

"I am not here." The boy's voice was very clear. "I am not."

"You are a rascal," said Mma. Ramotswe. "How can you say you are not there? Who is speaking if it is not you?"

There was a further silence, and then the branches of a bush parted and the small boy crawled out.

"He killed a hoopoe with his catapult," whispered Mr. J.L.B. Matekoni. "I saw it."

Mma. Ramotswe drew in her breath as the boy approached her, his head down, looking steadfastly at the ground.

"Go to your room, Puso," she said. "Go to your room and stay there until we call you."

The boy looked up. His face was streaked with tears.

"I hate you," he said. Then he turned to Mr. J.L.B. Matekoni. "And I hate you, too."

The words seemed to hang in the air between them, but the boy now dashed past the two astonished adults, running back towards the house, not looking back at Mma. Ramotswe and Mr. J.L.B. Matekoni as he ran.

CHAPTER FOUR

TRUST YOUR AFFAIRS TO A MAN

NOTHING SEEMED to be going well for Mma. Ramotswe. Firstly, there was that distressing evening with the children—Motholeli being bullied and the boy behaving in that troubling way, shooting a hoopoe and then remaining mute for the rest of the evening. There were matters still to be sorted out for Motholeli, of course, but at least she had cheered up after their talk; with the boy it had been different. He had just shut them out, refusing to eat, and it seemed that nothing they could say would make any difference. They had not attempted to punish him over the hoopoe, and one might have thought that he would be grateful for that, but he was not. Did he really hate them? And, if he did, why should he do so when all they had offered him was love and support? Was this how orphan children behaved? Mma. Ramotswe knew that children who were damaged in their early years could be very difficult; and this boy, when all was said and done, had actually been buried alive as a baby. Something like that could leave a mark; indeed, it would have been surprising had it not. But why should he suddenly turn on them like that when he had seemed to be quite happy before? That was puzzling. She would have to go and see Mma. Potokwani at the orphan farm and seek her advice. There was nothing that Mma. Potokwani did not know about children and their behaviour.

But that was not all. There had been a development which could threaten the No. 1 Ladies' Detective Agency itself, unless something was done; and nothing, it seemed, could be done. It was Mma. Makutsi who broke the news on the morning after the disturbing events at Zebra Drive.

"I have very bad news," said Mma. Makutsi when Mma. Ramotswe arrived at the office. "I have been sitting here for the last hour, wanting to cry."

Mma. Ramotswe looked at her assistant. She was not sure if she could take more trauma after last night; she felt raw from her engagement with the children's problems, and she had been look-ing forward to a quiet day. It would not matter if there were no clients that day; in fact, it would be better if there were no clients at all. It was difficult enough having one's own problems to sort out, let alone having to attend to the problems of others.

"Do you really have to tell me?" asked Mma. Ramotswe. "I am not in a mood for problems."

Mma. Makutsi pursed her lips. "This is very important, Mma.," she said severely, as if lecturing one who was being completely irre-sponsible. "I cannot pretend that I have not seen what I have seen."

Mma. Ramotswe sat down at her desk and looked across at Mma. Makutsi.

"In that case," she said, "you had better tell me. What has happened?"

Mma. Makutsi took off her spectacles and polished them on the hem of her skirt.

"Well," she said, "yesterday afternoon, as you may remember, Mma., I left a little bit early. At four o'clock."

Mma. Ramotswe nodded. "You said that you had to go shop-ping."

"Yes," said Mma. Makutsi. "And I did go shopping. I went up to the Broadhurst shops. There is a shop there that sells stockings very cheaply. I wanted to go there."

Mma. Ramotswe smiled. "It is always best to go after bargains. I always do that."

Mma. Makutsi acknowledged the remark but pressed on. "There is a shop there—or there used to be a shop there—that sold cups and saucers. You may remember it. The owner went away and they closed it down. Do you remember?"

Mma. Ramotswe did. She had bought a birthday present for somebody there, a large cup with a picture of a horse on it, and the handle had fallen off almost immediately.

"That place was empty for a while," said Mma. Makutsi. "But when I went up there yesterday afternoon and walked past it, just before half past four, I saw a new person putting up a sign outside the shop. And I saw some new furniture through the window. Brand-new office furniture."

She glanced around at the shabby furniture with which their own office was filled: the old grey filing cabinet with one drawer that did not work properly; the desks with their uneven surfaces; the rickety chairs. Mma. Ramotswe intercepted the glance and anticipated what was coming. There was going to be a request for new furniture. Mma. Makutsi must have spoken to somebody up there at Broadhurst and had been told of bargains to be had. But it would be impossible. The business was losing money as it was; it was only because of the connection with Tlokweng Road Speedy Motors and the paying of Mma. Makutsi's salary through that side of the business that they managed to continue trading at all. If it were not for Mr. J.L.B. Matekoni, they would have had to close down some months ago.

Mma. Ramotswe raised a hand. "I'm sorry, Mma. Makutsi,"

she said. "We cannot buy new equipment here. We simply don't have the money."

Mma. Makutsi stared at her. "That was not what I was going to say," she protested. "I was going to say something quite different." She paused, so that Mma. Ramotswe might feel suitably guilty for her unwarranted assumption.

"I'm sorry," said Mma. Ramotswe. "Tell me what you saw."

"A new detective agency," said Mma. Makutsi. "As large as life. It calls itself the Satisfaction Guaranteed Detective Agency."

Mma. Makutsi folded her arms, watching the effect of her words upon her employer. Mma. Ramotswe narrowed her eyes. This was dramatic news indeed. She had become so used to being the only private detective in town, indeed in the whole country, that it had never occurred to her there would be competition. This was the news that she least wished to hear, and for a moment she was tempted to throw her hands in the air and announce that she was giving up. But that was a passing thought, and no more than that. Mma. Ramotswe was not one to give up that easily, and even if it was discouraging to have orphan problems at home and a shortage of work at the agency, this was no reason to abandon the business. So she squared her shoulders and smiled at Mma. Makutsi.

"Every business must expect competition," she said. "We are no different. We cannot expect to have it all our own way forever, can we?"

Mma. Makutsi looked doubtful. "No," she said at last. "We learned about that at the Botswana Secretarial College. It's called the principle of competition."

"Oh," said Mma. Ramotswe. "And what does this principle say?"

Mma. Makutsi looked momentarily flustered. She had received ninety-seven percent in the final examinations at the

Botswana Secretarial College—that was well-known—but she had never been examined on the principle of competition, as far as she could recall.

"It means that there is competition," she pronounced. "You don't just have one business. There will always be more than one business."

"That is true," said Mma. Ramotswe.

"So that means that if one business does well, then there will be other businesses which will try to do well, too," Mma. Makutsi went on, warming to her theme. "There is nothing that can be done about it. In fact, it is healthy."

Mma. Ramotswe was not convinced. "Healthy enough to take away all our business," she said.

Mma. Makutsi nodded. "But we also learned that you have to know what the competition is. I remember them saying that."

Mma. Ramotswe agreed, and, encouraged, Mma. Makutsi continued. "We need to do some detective work for ourselves," she said. "We need to go and take a look at these new people and see what they are up to. Then we will know what the competition is."

Mma. Ramotswe reached for the key to her tiny white van.

"You are right, Mma. Makutsi," she said. "We need to go and introduce ourselves to these new detectives. Then we'll know just how clever they are."

"Yes," said Mma. Makutsi. "And there's one other thing. These new detectives are not ladies, like ourselves. These are men."

"Ah," said Mma. Ramotswe. "That is a good thing, and a bad thing, too."

IT WAS not hard to find the Satisfaction Guaranteed Detective Agency. A large sign, very similar to the one which had appeared outside the original premises of the No. 1 Ladies' Detective Agency, announced the name of the business and showed a picture of a smiling man behind a desk, hands folded, and clearly satisfied. Then, underneath this picture, was painted in large red letters: Experienced staff. Ex-CID. Ex–New York. Ex-cellent!

Mma. Ramotswe parked the tiny white van on the opposite side of the street, under a convenient acacia tree.

"So!" she said, her voice lowered, although nobody could possibly hear them. "So that is the competition."

Mma. Makutsi, who was sitting in the passenger seat, leaned forward to be able to see past Mma. Ramotswe. Her employer was a large lady—traditionally built, as she described herself—and it was not easy to get a good view of the offending sign.

"Ex-CID," said Mma. Ramotswe. "A retired policeman then. That is not good news for us. People will love the idea of taking their problems to a retired policeman."

"And ex–New York," said Mma. Makutsi admiringly. "That will impress people a great deal. They have seen films about New York detectives and they know how good they are."

Mma. Ramotswe cast a glance at Mma. Makutsi. "Do you mean Superman?" she asked.

"Yes," said Mma. Makutsi. "That sort of thing. Superman."

Mma. Ramotswe opened her mouth to say something to her assistant but then stopped. She was well aware of Mma. Makutsi's academic achievements at the Botswana Secretarial College—she could hardly avoid the framed certificate to that effect hanging above Mma. Makutsi's desk—but sometimes she thought her extraordinarily naive. Superman indeed! Why anybody above, well, the age of six or seven *at the most* should be interested in such nonsense quite escaped her. And yet they did show an interest; when films like that came to the cinema in town, the one owned by the rich man with a house near Nyerere Drive, there were always crowds of people who were prepared to pay for the seats. Of course some of these were courting couples, who would not necessarily be interested in what was happening on the screen, but others appeared to go for the films themselves.

There was no point in arguing about Superman with Mma. Makutsi. Whoever had opened this agency, even if they were really ex–New York, would hardly be Superman.

"We'll go in and introduce ourselves," said Mma. Ramotswe. "I can see somebody inside. They are already at work."

"On some big important case," observed Mma. Makutsi ruefully.

"Perhaps," said Mma. Ramotswe. "But then again, perhaps not. When people drive past the No. 1 Ladies' Detective Agency and see us inside, they may think that we're working on a big important case. Yet most of the time, as you know, we are only sitting there drinking bush tea and reading the Botswana Daily News. So you see that appearances can be deceptive."

Mma. Makutsi thought that this was rather too self-effacing. It was true that they were not particularly busy at present, and it was also true that a fair amount of bush tea was consumed in the office, but it was not always like that. There were times when they were very busy and the passerby would have been quite correct in making the assumption that the office was a hive of activity. So Mma. Ramotswe was wrong; but there was no point in arguing with Mma. Ramotswe, who seemed to be in a rather defeatist mood. Something was happening at home, thought Mma. Makutsi, because it was so unlike her to be anything but optimistic.

They crossed the road and approached the door of the small shop which now housed the Satisfaction Guaranteed Detective Agency. The front was largely taken up by a glass display window, behind which a screen prevented the passerby from seeing more than the heads of the people working within. In the window was a framed picture of a group of men standing together outside a rather impressive-looking official building. The men were all wearing wide-brimmed hats which shaded their faces and made it impossible to distinguish their features.

"Not a good photograph," muttered Mma. Ramotswe to Mma. Makutsi. "Worse than useless."

The door itself, which was half glass-fronted, bore a hand-written sign: Please Enter. No Need to Knock. But Mma. Ramotswe, who believed in the traditional values—one of which was always to knock and call out *Ko Ko!* before one entered—knocked at the door before pushing it open.

"No need to knock, Mma.," said a man sitting behind a desk. "Just come in."

"I always knock, Rra.," said Mma. Ramotswe. "It is the right thing to do."

The man smiled. "In my business," he said, "it's not always a good idea to knock. It warns people to stop whatever they're doing."

Mma. Ramotswe laughed at the joke. "And one would not want that!"

"No, indeed," said the man. "But as you see, I am doing nothing bad. What a pity! I am just sitting here waiting for two beautiful ladies like you to come in and see me."

Mma. Ramotswe glanced very quickly at Mma. Makutsi before she replied. "You are a very kind man, Rra.," she said. "I am not called beautiful every day. It is nice when that happens."

The man behind the desk made a self-deprecating gesture. "When you are a detective, Mma., you get used to observing things. I saw you coming in, and the first thing I said to myself was: *Two very, very beautiful ladies coming in the door. This is your lucky day. . . ."* He stopped, and then, rising to his feet and sitting down again almost immediately, he put the palm of a hand to his forehead.

"But, Mma., what am I saying! You are Mma. Ramotswe, aren't you? The No. 1 Ladies' Detective Agency? I have seen your picture in the newspaper, and here I am telling you all about being a detective! And all the time it is you and Mma. . . . Mma. . . ."

"Makutsi," said Mma. Makutsi. "I am an assistant detective at the No. 1 Ladies' Detective Agency. I was at the Botswana Secretarial College before—"

The man nodded, cutting her short. "Oh, that place. Yes."

Mma. Ramotswe noticed the effect which this had on Mma. Makutsi. It was as if somebody had applied an electric wire to her skin.

"It is a fine college," said Mma. Ramotswe quickly, and then, to change the subject, "But what is your name, Rra.?"

"I am Mr. Buthelezi," said the man, reaching out to shake hands. "Cephas Buthelezi. Ex-CID."

Mma. Ramotswe took his hand and shook it, as did Mma. Makutsi, reluctantly in her case. Then, invited to sit down by Mr. Buthelezi, they lowered themselves gingerly onto the shiny new chairs in front of his desk.

"Buthelezi is a famous name," said Mma. Ramotswe. "Are you of the same family as he is?"

Mr. Buthelezi laughed. "Or might one say, is he of the same family as I am? Ha, ha!"

Mma. Ramotswe waited a moment. "Well, is he?" she asked.

Mr. Buthelezi reached for a packet of cigarettes on his desk and extracted one.

"Many people are called Buthelezi," he said. "And many people are not. People are also called Nkomo or Ramaphosa or whatever.

That does not make them a real Nkomo or a real Ramaphosa, does it? There are many names, are there not?"

Mma. Ramotswe nodded her agreement. "That is true, Rra. There are many names."

Mr. Buthelezi lit his cigarette. He had not offered his guests one—not that they smoked—but the lack of consideration had been noted, at least by Mma. Makutsi, who, after the slighting reference to the Botswana Secretarial College, was looking for reasons to damn their newly discovered competitor.

Mma. Ramotswe had been waiting for an answer to her question but now realised that one would not be forthcoming. "Of course," she said, "that is a Zulu name, is it not? You are from that part of the world, Rra.?"

Mr. Buthelezi picked a fragment of tobacco from his front teeth.

"My late father was a Zulu from Natal," he said. "But my late mother was from here, a Motswana. She met my father when she was working over the border, in South Africa. She sent me to school in Botswana, and then, when I had finished school, I went back to live with them in South Africa. That is when I joined the CID in Johannesburg. Now I am back in my mother's country."

"And I see on your sign that you have lived in New York, too," said Mma. Ramotswe. "You have had a busy life, Rra.!"

Mr. Buthelezi looked away, as if remembering a rich and varied life. "Yes, New York. I have been in New York."

"Did you like living there, Rra.?" asked Mma. Makutsi. "I have always wanted to go to New York."

"New York is a very large city," said Mr. Buthelezi. "My God! Wow! There are many buildings there."

"But how long did you live there?" asked Mma. Makutsi. "Were you there for many years?"

"Not many years," said Mr. Buthelezi.

"How long?" asked Mma. Makutsi.

"You are very interested in New York, Mma.," said Mr. Buthelezi. "You should go there yourself. Don't just get my view of it. See the place with your own eyes. Wow!"

For a few moments there was a silence, with Mma. Makutsi's unanswered question hanging in the air: how long? Mr. Buthelezi drew on his cigarette and blew the smoke up towards the ceiling. He seemed comfortable enough with the silence, but after a while he reached forward and passed a small leaflet to Mma. Ramotswe.

"This is my brochure, Mma.," he said. "I am happy for you to see it. I do not mind that there is more than one detective agency in this town. It's growing so quickly, isn't it? There is work for two of us." *And what about me?* thought Mma. Makutsi. *What about me? Are there not three of us, or am I just a nothing in your eyes?*

Mma. Ramotswe took the cheaply printed brochure. There was a picture of Mr. Buthelezi on the front, sitting at a different desk and looking rather formal. She turned the page. Again there was a picture of Mr. Buthelezi, this time standing beside a black car, with indistinct tall buildings in the background. The middle ground, which was oddly hazy, appeared to be waste ground of some sort, and there were no other figures in the photograph, which was labelled underneath, *New York.*

She looked at the text opposite the picture. *Is something troubling you?* it read. *Is your husband coming home late and smelling of ladies' perfume? Is one of your employees stealing your business secrets? Don't take any chances! Entrust your enquiries to a MAN!*

The effect of this on Mma. Ramotswe was similar to the effect which the earlier remark about the Botswana Secretarial College had produced on Mma. Makutsi. Silently she passed the brochure to her assistant, who adjusted her glasses to read it.

"It has been very good to meet you, Rra.," said Mma.

Ramotswe, struggling with the words. Insincerity had never come easily to her, but good manners required it on occasion, even if a superhuman effort was needed. "We must meet again soon so that we can discuss our cases together."

Mr. Buthelezi beamed with pleasure. "That would be very good, Mma.," he said. "You and me talking about professional matters . . ."

"And Mma. Makutsi," said Mma. Ramotswe.

"Of course," said Mr. Buthelezi, glancing quickly, and dismissively, at his other visitor.

Mma. Makutsi had handed the brochure back to Mr. Buthelezi, who insisted that they keep it. Then the two women stood up, took their leave politely, if rather coldly, and left the shop, closing the door perhaps rather too firmly behind them. Once outside, they crossed the road in complete silence, and it was not until Mma. Ramotswe had turned the tiny white van round and started to head for home that anything was said.

"So!" said Mma. Ramotswe.

Mma. Makutsi searched for something to say but could think of nothing that fitted the occasion; nothing that summed up her outrage at the way in which the Botswana Secretarial College had been referred to as *that place*. So she said "So," too, and left it at that.

CHAPTER FIVE

THE TALKING CURE

THEY RETURNED to the office in silence. Mma. Makutsi wanted to talk, but one look at Mma. Ramotswe, sitting behind the wheel of the tiny white van, her face set in an uncharacteristic scowl, persuaded her that if there was to be any discussion of their encounter with Mr. Buthelezi, then this would have to come later. There could be no doubt, of course, of what Mma. Ramotswe thought about their new colleague—if one could call him that. How dare he sit there and speak to Mma. Ramotswe, the doyenne of the profession of private enquiry agent in Botswana, in that condescending fashion, as if he had all the experience and she were the newcomer. And then there was the boastful brochure, which Mma. Makutsi now clutched in her hands, resisting all temptation to crunch it into a ball and throw it out of the window of the tiny white van. It was reasonable enough, of course, for people to wish to speak to a man, if that is what they wanted, but that did not mean that a man would be better. Trust your enquiries to a man indeed! The No. 1 Ladies' Detective Agency, as they had made abundantly clear from the very beginning, was not merely a service provided for ladies by ladies; it was a service for everybody, men and women equally. And the title made no claim to the special talents of ladies in private detection (although one could make that case if one sat down to it); all it implied was that this was a detective agency that happened to be run by ladies.

Mma. Ramotswe parked the tiny white van directly behind the garage, outside the back door of the building that they shared with Tlokweng Road Speedy Motors. Mr. J.L.B. Matekoni was busy in the inspection pit, peering up at the chassis of a battered blue minibus and showing something to one of the apprentices beside him. He waved cheerfully, and Mma. Ramotswe acknowledged his greeting, but she did not walk over to chat with him, as she normally would have done. Instead, both she and Mma. Makutsi went directly into the agency and sat down at their desks in indignant silence.

Mma. Makutsi had garage bills to attend to, and she busied herself with these. Mma. Ramotswe, who sat on the committee of the Anglican Cathedral Women's League for Better Housing, had the minutes of a meeting to read through and a draft to prepare of a letter to the Ministry of Housing. She immersed herself in these tasks, but she found it difficult to concentrate, and after twenty minutes or so of saying the wrong thing to the deputy minister, and being unable to find the right words, she rose to her feet and went outside.

It was a comfortable time of year, immediately after the worst of the heat and before the winter set in. Not that the country had much of a winter. The nights could get chilly, of course, with that dry cold that could penetrate to the very bones, but the winter days were usually sunny and clear, with air that one could almost drink, so pure and fresh it was; air with a hint of wood smoke; air that filled one with gratitude that one was here, in this place, and nowhere else. This time of year, when the grass was already turning brown but there were still patches of green, was perfect, in Mma. Ramotswe's view. Now she stood outside, under one of the acacia trees, looking towards Tlokweng, watching a small group of donkeys cropping the grass beside the road. Her anger had largely passed, and watching the patient, unassuming donkeys helped restore her sense of perspective. The children's difficulties were not really serious; small boys could behave in peculiar ways (just like men), and as for Motholeli, bullying was an inevitable, universal problem. She would discuss this with Mma. Potokwani, who would tell her exactly what to do.

Mr. Buthelezi was a rather more serious matter, but then again, was he really that much of a threat? He was bombastic and pleased with himself, but that did not mean he would take business away from her. People did not want bluster when they were worried about something; they wanted good sense and caution. Those ridiculous photographs of him would surely put people off. People could tell the difference, could they not, between fantasy and reality? As Clovis Andersen pointed out in *The Principles of Private Detection,* anybody who went into the profession thinking that it was glamorous because they had read books or seen films about it was fundamentally misguided. Of course Mr. Buthelezi would never have read Clovis Andersen (*I should have asked him directly,* thought Mma. Ramotswe; *that would have put him in place*).

She turned away from the road and looked away, down to the stand of eucalyptus trees that had been planted years ago, when Gaborone was still called Chief Gaborone's Place, and which had established itself as a forest. She was fearful of this forest, for some reason, and never walked there alone. It was a sad place, she thought, with its tall red-brown termite mounds and its paths that went to nobody's house but merely petered out in bark-littered clearings. Cattle moved through the trees, and she could hear their bells now but turned away with a shiver. That was not a good place.

The donkeys had wandered onto the road and were standing

still, wondering whether to cross or not. A boy shouted at them and threw a stone to move them on, calling out their names: Broken Ear, Broken Ear! Thin One, Thin One! Come on, come on, move!

Which was Broken Ear, she wondered, as they all seemed to have fine ears, and none, now that one came to think of it, looked particularly thin. She was thinking of this, of the names which people give their animals, when a car turned off the road, circled Tlokweng Road Speedy Motors twice, and then drew up next to the tiny white van. Mma. Ramotswe watched as the driver, a tall, well-built man in his early forties, got out.

"Dumela, Mma.," he said as he walked over towards her. "Can you help me? I am looking for the No. 1 Ladies' Detective Agency."

Mma. Ramotswe realised that she must seem somewhat dreamy to him, standing there, staring at the donkeys; a woman who was perhaps not all there in the head. "That is me, Rra. I am sorry, I was thinking of something else." She pointed to the donkeys. "I was listening to the herd boy calling out the names of those donkeys. I was not paying attention."

The man chuckled. "And why should you? There's nothing wrong with watching donkeys, or cattle, for that matter. I love to watch cattle myself. I can look at them for hours."

"Who can't?" replied Mma. Ramotswe. "My father had a good eye for cattle. He could tell you a lot about a cow's owner just by looking at her."

"There are people like that," he agreed. "It is a great talent. Perhaps you can do it. You could be a cattle detective, asking the cattle to tell you things."

Mma. Ramotswe laughed. She had immediately taken to this man, whoever he was; he was the opposite of Mr. Buthelezi. You could not imagine this man being photographed in a wide-brimmed hat.

"I must tell you my name," said the man. "I am Molefelo, and I come from Lobatse. I am a civil engineer, but I have a hotel down there, too. I used to build things, but now I just sit in an office and run them. It is not as much fun, I'm afraid."

Mma. Ramotswe listened politely. She had heard vaguely of Mr. Molefelo, she thought. She knew Lobatse, and she had probably been to his hotel once or twice with Mr. J.L.B. Matekoni when they had gone down there together to visit her cousin. In fact, the last time she had been there, she had eaten a meal which had made her very ill; but this was not the time to mention that, she thought.

"We can go into the office," she said, pointing to the door. "It will be more comfortable to sit down. My assistant will make us tea and we can talk."

Mr. Molefelo glanced towards the door of the agency, where Mma. Makutsi could be seen, peering out at them.

"I wonder if we could stay outside," he said hesitantly. "It is such a pleasant day and. . . ." He paused before continuing. "Actually, Mma., what I have to say is very private. Very, very private. I wonder if we could talk about it outside? We could take a walk, perhaps. I could talk to you while we were walking."

Mma. Ramotswe had encountered embarrassment before in her clients and understood that it was often no use trying to reassure them. If there was something which was really private, the presence of another often inhibited them. Of course, there was nothing—or almost nothing—that she had not heard. Nothing would astonish her, although there were occasions on which she marvelled at the ability people had to complicate their lives.

"I'm happy to go for a walk," she said to Mr. Molefelo. "I will just tell my assistant that I am going, and then I am ready."

THEY WALKED along a path that led back from the garage in the direction of the dam. There were thorn bushes and the sweet smell of grazing cattle. As they walked, Mr. Molefelo talked, and Mma. Ramotswe listened.

"You may wonder, Mma., why I am telling you this, but I think you should know that I am a man who has changed. Something happened to me two months ago which has made me think about everything, about my whole life and how I've led it, and about how I should lead the rest of it. Do you know what I'm talking about?"

"You are not talking to a particularly bad man, or anything like that. You are talking to a man who is probably much like other men. Just an average sort of man. There are thousands of men like me in Botswana. Ordinary men. Not very clever and not very stupid. Just ordinary men."

"You are being modest," interrupted Mma. Ramotswe. "You are an engineer, aren't you? That is a clever thing to be."

"Not really. You have to be able to do mathematics and technical drawing, maybe. But beyond that, it's mostly common sense." He was silent for a moment before continuing. "But that's not the point about being ordinary. The point about being ordinary is that the average man does some bad things in his life and some good things. There are probably no men who have done no bad things. Probably not one."

"Nor women," said Mma. Ramotswe. "Women are just as bad as men. Sometimes they are worse."

"I wouldn't know about that," said Mr. Molefelo. "I do not know many women very well. I do not know how women behave. But that is not the point. I was talking about men, and I think I do know how men behave."

"You have done a bad thing?" asked Mma. Ramotswe bluntly. "Is that what you're trying to say?"

Mr. Molefelo nodded. "I have. But don't worry, it was not too bad—I haven't killed anybody or anything like that. I'll tell you about the bad thing I did—although I haven't told anybody else, you know. But first I should like to tell you about what happened a few months ago. Then you will understand why I want to talk to you.

"As I told you, I have a hotel down in Lobatse. This has done quite well—it is a good place for weddings—and I have used the money I made from it to buy land. I bought land down near the border with Namibia, right down there. It takes me four hours' driving from Lobatse to get there, and so I can't go down every week. I have a man, though, who looks after it for me, and there are some families who live on the land and do work for me."

"And this man, is he good with cattle? That is very important," said Mma. Ramotswe.

"Yes, he is good with cattle. But he is also good with ostriches. I have a good flock of ostriches down there and some fine birds. Big ones. Strong. It's a good place for ostriches."

Mma. Ramotswe did not know about ostriches. She had seen them, of course, and she knew that many people were keen on them. But in her mind, they were a poor substitute for cattle. She imagined a Botswana covered with ostriches rather than cattle. What a strange place that would be; undignified, really.

"My ostriches are well known for their good meat," Mr. Molefelo went on. "But they are also good breeders. I have one who is very kind to the hens and has many children. He is a very fine ostrich, and I keep him in a special paddock so that he does not fight. I have seen him kick, you know. Ow! If he kicked a man, he would divide him in two. I'm not exaggerating. Two pieces. Down the middle."

"I shall be very careful," said Mma. Ramotswe.

"I saw a man kicked by an ostrich once. He was the brother of one of the men who works on my farm, and he was not very strong. A long time ago, when he was a child, he was trodden upon by some cattle and hurt his back. He did not grow up straight, because his spine was twisted. So he could not do much work. Then he got TB, and that made him even worse. All that coughing, I suppose, makes you very weak.

"He came to see his brother one day, and they gave him some beer, although this weak man was not used to drinking. He liked the beer, and it made him feel brave for once in his life. So he went over to the ostrich pen and climbed over the tall fence that we use to keep the ostriches in. There was an ostrich nearby who was watching him, and he was very surprised when a man ran up to him waving his arms. The ostrich tried to run away, but he caught his wing in the fence and was slow. So the man caught him, and that was when the ostrich kicked him.

"I had heard all this shouting when the man climbed over the fence, and I came to see what was happening. I saw him trying to seize the ostrich's tail feathers, and then I saw him going up in the air and landing down with a thump. He never got up, but lay there while the ostrich looked at him. And that was the end of that man."

Mma. Ramotswe looked down at the ground, thinking of this poor man with his twisted spine. "I am sorry to hear about that man," she said. "There are many sad things that happen, and sometimes we do not hear about them. All the time, there are these sad things that God sends Africa."

"Yes," said Mr. Molefelo. "You are right, Mma. The world is very cruel to us sometimes."

They walked on a few paces, thinking about what Mma. Ramotswe had said. Then Mr. Molefelo continued. "I must now tell you what happened to me just a few months ago. This is not just a story that I am telling you; it is so that you can understand why I have come to see you.

"I went down to my farm with my wife and my two sons. They are strong boys—one is this high and one is this high." He gestured with the palm of his hand held upwards; it was never a good idea to show the height of a person with the palm facing downwards, as this could push the spirit down. "We were going to stay there for a week, but something happened on the second night which changed that. Some men came to the farm from over the border. They came at night, riding on their horses. They were ostrich rustlers."

Mma. Ramotswe stopped and looked at Mr. Molefelo in astonishment.

"There are ostrich rustlers? They steal your ostriches?"

Mr. Molefelo nodded. "They are very dangerous men. They come in bands with their guns, and they chase the ostriches back over the border into Namibia. The Namibians say that they are trying to catch them, but there are never enough policemen. Never. They say they will look for them, but how do you find men like that who live out in the bush, in camps? They are like ghosts. They come and go at night, and you will find a ghost more easily than you will find those men. They are men who have no names, no family, nothing. They are like leopards.

"I was sleeping in the house when they came. I am not a heavy sleeper, and I heard a noise down in the ostrich paddocks. So I got out of bed to see whether there was some creature coming to eat the ostriches—a lion, perhaps, or a hyena. I took a big torch and my rifle, and I walked down the path that led from the house to the paddocks. I did not need to switch on the torch, as there was a very large moon, which made shadows on the ground.

"I had almost reached the paddock when I was suddenly

knocked to the ground. I dropped my rifle and my torch, and my face was in the dirt. I remember breathing the dust and coughing, and then I was kicked in the side, painfully, and a man pulled my head up and looked at me. He had a rifle in his hand—not my rifle—and he put the barrel at my head and said something to me. I did not understand him, as he was not speaking in Setswana. It may have been Hereto or one of the languages they speak over there. It could even have been Afrikaans, which quite a lot of them use down there, not just the Boers.

"I thought I was going to die, and so I thought of my sons. I wondered what would happen to them when they no longer had a father. Then I thought of my own father, for some reason, and I remembered walking with him through the bush, just as we are doing now, Mma., and talking to him about cattle. I thought that I would like to do that with my own sons, but I had been too busy, and now it was too late. These were strange thoughts. I was not thinking of myself but of other people."

Mma. Ramotswe stooped down to pick up an interesting-looking stick. "I can understand that," she said, examining the stick, "I'm sure that I would think the same."

But would she? She had never been in that position; she had never been in danger at all, really, and she had no idea what would go through her mind. She would like to imagine that she would think of her father, Obed Ramotswe, the Daddy, that great man; but perhaps if matters came to such a pass, the mind would do the wrong thing and start thinking about mundane issues, like the electricity bill. It would be sad to leave this life on such a note, worrying about whether the Botswana Electricity Corporation had been paid. The Botswana Electricity Corporation would never think about her, she was sure.

"This man was very rough. He pulled my head back. Then he made me sit up, with the gun still pointing at my head, while he called out to one of his friends. They came out of the shadows, on their horses, and they stood about me, with the horses breathing against me. They talked among themselves, and I realised that they were discussing whether or not to shoot me. I am sure that they were talking about this, although I could not understand their language.

"Then I saw a light and heard somebody in the distance call out in Setswana. It was one of my men, who must now have woken up and had shouted out to the others. This made the man who was holding me hit me on the side of the head with his rifle. Then he stood up and ran over to a tree where he had tied his horse. There was more shouting from my men, and I heard them start the engine of the truck. One of the men who had surrounded me shouted out something to the others, and they rode off. I was left alone, feeling the blood run down the side of my face. I still have a scar, which you can see, look, just here between my cheek and my ear. That is my reminder of what happened."

"You were a lucky man to have escaped," said Mma. Ramotswe. "They could easily have shot you. If you weren't here talking to me, I would have thought the story ended quite differently."

Mr. Molefelo smiled. "I thought that, too. But it did not. And I was able to go back to see my wife and my sons, who started to cry when they saw their father with blood streaming down his face. And I was crying, too, I think, and shaking all over like a dog who's been thrown in the water. And I was like this for more than a day, I think. I was very ashamed. A man should not behave like that. But I was like a frightened little boy.

"We went back to Lobatse so that I could see one of the doctors there who knew how to stitch up faces. He gave me injections and drew the wound together. Then I went back to work and tried to forget about what had happened. But I could not,

Mma. I kept thinking about what this meant for my life. I know that this may sound strange to you, but it made me think about everything I had done. It made me weigh up my life. And it made me want to tie things up, so that next time—and I hope there will not be a next time—the next time I faced death like that, I could think: *I have set my life in order.*"

"That is a very good idea," said Mma. Ramotswe. "We should all do that, I think. But we never do. For example, my electricity bill—"

"Those are small things," Mr. Molefelo interjected. "Bills and debts are nothing, really. What really counts are the things that you have done to people. That is what counts. And that is why I've come to see you, Mma. I want to confess. I do not go to the Catholic Church, where you can sit in a box and tell the priest all about the things you have done. I cannot do that. But I want to talk to somebody, and that is why I have come to see you."

Mma. Ramotswe nodded. She understood. Shortly after opening the No. 1 Ladies' Detective Agency, she had discovered that part of her role would be to listen to people and to help them unburden themselves of their past. And indeed her subsequent reading of Clovis Andersen had confirmed this. *Be gentle,* he had written. *Many of the people who will come to see you are injured in spirit. They need to talk about things that have hurt them, or about things that they have done. Do not sit in judgement on them, but listen. Just listen.*

They had reached a place where the path dipped down into a dried-up watercourse. There was a termite mound to one side of it, and on the other, a small expanse of rock rising out of the red earth. There was the chewed-up pith of sugarcane lying to the side of the path and a fragment of broken blue glass, which caught the sun. Not far away a goat was standing on its hind legs, nibbling at the less accessible leaves of a shrub. It was a good place to sit and listen, under a sky that had seen so much and heard so much that one more wicked deed would surely make no difference. Sins, thought Mma. Ramotswe, are darker and more powerful when contemplated within confining walls. Out in the open, under such a sky as this, misdeeds were reduced to their natural proportions—small, mean things that could be faced quite openly, sorted, and folded away.

CHAPTER SIX

OLD TYPEWRITERS, GATHERING DUST

MMA. MAKUTSI watched Mma. Ramotswe set off for her walk with Mr. Molefelo and said to herself: "This is one of the limitations of being only an assistant detective. I miss the important things. I hear about the clients at one remove. I am really just a secretary, not an assistant detective." And, turning to the pile of garage bills which was now ready for despatch, she thought: "I am not really an assistant garage manager, either; I am a garage secretary, which is a different thing altogether."

She rose from her desk to make herself a cup of bush tea. Even if a client had arrived—and there was no guarantee that the consultation taking place on the walk would mature into a full-scale, paid investigation—the future of the agency, and of her job, looked doubtful. There was also the question of money. She knew that Mma. Ramotswe and Mr. J.L.B. Matekoni paid her as generously as they could, but after she had paid her increasingly expensive rent and sent money home to her parents and aunts in Bobonong, there was virtually nothing left for her to spend on herself. She was aware of the fact that some of her dresses were wearing thin and that her shoes would need resoling before too long. She did her best to keep her appearance smart, but it was difficult on a tight budget. At the moment, all that she had in her savings account was two hundred and thirty-eight pula and forty-five thebe. That would not be enough for a pair of good new shoes or a couple of dresses. And once she had spent that, there would be nothing left to buy the medicines that she might need for her brother.

Mma. Makutsi realised that the only way of improving her situation was to take on extra work in her spare time. The driving school had been a good idea, but the more she thought about it, the more she realised that it would not work. She imagined what would happen if she were to speak about it to Mr. J.L.B. Matekoni. He would be supportive, of course, but she could hear his response, even before he made it.

"The insurance will be too expensive," he would point out. "If you are going to let learners drive a car, you have to pay a very high premium. The insurance companies know that they will crash."

He would tell her what the extra premium was likely to be, and she would be shocked by the figure. If that was what she would have to pay, then her earlier calculations were all wrong. They would have to charge very much more for each lesson, and that would cut out any advantage they might have over the large driving schools, which could use economies of scale. So the idea, which had seemed to offer a real prospect of extra money, would have to be abandoned, and she would have to start thinking of alternatives.

It was while she was typing a letter to one of the garage's recalcitrant debtors that the idea occurred to her. It was such a strikingly good idea that it took over her train of thought and became incorporated in the letter itself:

"Dear Sir," she typed, "We have written to you before on 25/11 and 18/12 and 14/2 about the outstanding sum of five hundred and twenty-two pula in respect of the repair of your vehicle. We note that you have not paid this sum and we have therefore no alternative but to. . . . Isn't it an interesting thing that most typists are women? When I was at the Botswana Secretarial College, it was only women, and yet men have to type if they want to use computers, which they do if they are engineers or businessmen or work in banks. I have seen them sitting in banks trying to type with one finger and wasting a lot of time. Why do they not learn to type properly? The answer to that is that they are ashamed to say they cannot type and they do not want to go and have to learn with a class full of girls. They are worried that the girls would be better at typing than they are! And they would be! Even those useless girls who only got fifty percent at the college. Even they would be better than men. So why not have a special class for men—a typing school for men? They could come after work and learn to type with other men. We could hold this class in a church hall, perhaps, so that when the men came to it, people would think that they were just going to a church meeting. I could teach it myself. I would be the principal and would give the men a special certificate at the end of the course. This is to certify that Mr. So-and-So completed the course on typing for men and is now a proficient typist. Signed, Grace P. Makutsi, Principal, Kalahari Typing School for Men."

She finished typing the letter and drew it from the machine with a flourish. She was astonished at the way in which the words had flowed from her, and by the completeness, the utter rightness, of the business plan which the letter contained. Reading over it again, she reflected on the fundamental insight into male psychology which had sprung, unannounced, from the typewriter keys. Of course it was right that men did not like to see women doing things better than they did; this was something which every girl learned at an early age. She remembered how her brothers had been unable to bear losing any game to her or one of her sisters. They had to win, and if there was any sign that they might lose, the game would be abandoned on some pretext or other. And this was no different from adult life.

Typing, of course, was a special case. Not only was there male anxiety about being bettered by women in the operation of a machine (men liked to think that they were the ones who understood how to use machines), but there was the additional embarrassment for them of being seen to do something which many people viewed as a woman's activity. Men did not like to be secretaries and had invented a special word for men who had to do any of that sort of work. They called themselves clerks. But what was the difference between a clerk and a secretary? One wore trousers and one wore a dress.

Mma. Makutsi was convinced of the workability of her idea but realised there were many obstacles that would need to be overcome. First and foremost of these was a fundamental issue of what she had been taught at the Botswana Secretarial College to call capitalisation, but which, in simple language, meant money. Her capital was the grand total of two hundred and thirty eight pula and forty-five thebe, and that would buy, at the most, one secondhand typewriter. For a class of ten, she would need ten typewriters, which, at four hundred pula each, came to four thousand pula. This was a fabulous sum which would take her years to save. And even if she were able to borrow it from the bank, interest rates were such that all the fees from the students would go in payments. Not that the bank would lend to her in the first place, with no track record of profit and no security, not even one cow, for the loan.

There seemed no way round this brute fact of economic existence. To make money, one needed to have money in the first place. That was why those who had came by more and more. Mma. Ramotswe was an example of this. Although she was always very modest about her circumstances, she had started with the great advantage of being able to sell all those cattle left to her by her father, just at a time when the price of cattle had shot up. And she had inherited his savings, too, which had been wisely placed in a part share of a store and a piece of ground. The piece of ground, it turned out, had been exactly where a company needed to build a depot on the edge of Gaborone, and that had driven the price up to unimaginable levels. All this had enabled Mma. Ramotswe to buy the house in Zebra Drive and to set up the No. 1 Ladies' Detective Agency. That was why Mma. Ramotswe was the owner and she was the employee, and nothing, it seemed, would change that. Of course, she could marry a man with money, but what man with money would even look at her when there were all those glamorous girls around? Really, it was all very bleak.

Typewriters! Who had a large supply of old, partly unworkable typewriters gathering dust in a storeroom? The Botswana Secretarial College!

Mma. Makutsi picked up the telephone. There was a rule that personal calls from the garage and the agency were not allowed ("This is not directed against you," Mma. Ramotswe had said, "it's those apprentices. Imagine if they were able to speak on the phone from work to all those girls. We would not be able to pay the bill, or even half of it"). This was different. This was work, even if a sideline.

She dialled the number of the college and politely enquired after the health of the telephonist at the other end before she asked to speak to the assistant principal, Mma. Manapotsi. She knew Mma. Manapotsi well and often chatted with her if they met in town.

"We have always been so proud of you," said Mma. Manapotsi. "Ninety-seven percent! I shall never forget that. We still haven't had any other girl, not a single one, who has managed more than eighty-five percent. Your name is secure in the annals of the college! We are so proud."

"But you must also be proud of your son," Mma. Makutsi would remind her. Mma. Manapotsi's son, Harry, was a successful footballer, a member of the Zebras team and famous for scoring a crucial goal in a match against the Bulawayo Dynamos the previous year. He was an inveterate ladies' man, as many of these footballers were, and his hair was always covered with a curious sticky gel, for the benefit of ladies, Mma. Makutsi assumed. But his mother was proud of him, as any mother would be of a son who was capable of bringing crowds to their feet.

When Mma. Manapotsi was put on the line, they exchanged warm greetings before Mma. Makutsi broached the subject of the typewriters. As she spoke, she stood on her toe under the desk, just for luck. They might have thrown the old typewriters out by now, or had them repaired and put back into service.

She explained that she was hoping to start a small typing class and that she would be prepared to pay for the rental of the typewriters, even if they did not work perfectly.

"But of course," said Mma. Manapotsi. "Why not? Those old machines are useless, and we need to clear the space. You could have them in exchange for. . . ."

Mma. Makutsi thought of her savings and imagined the savings book with a row of noughts in every column.

"For an offer to come and talk to the girls now and then," went on Mma. Manapotsi. "I was thinking of introducing a new part of the curriculum. Talks from distinguished graduates on what to expect in the working world. You could be the first speaker."

Mma. Makutsi accepted the offer with alacrity.

"There are a dozen machines or so," said Mma. Manapotsi.

"They don't work properly, you know. They go qwertyui** rather than qwertyuiop. Some of them even go qop."

"I don't mind," said Mma. Makutsi. "They're only for men."

"Well, that's all right then," said Mma. Manapotsi.

MMA. MAKUTSI replaced the receiver on its cradle and then rose from her desk. She glanced through the open door that led into the garage; nobody was watching. Slowly, she began to gyrate round the office in celebratory dance, ululating quietly as she did so, her right hand moving back and forward before her mouth. It was a victory dance. The Kalahari Typing School for Men had just been born; her first business, her very own idea. It would work— she had no doubt of that—and it would solve all her problems. The men would come flocking, all eager to learn the vital skill, and the money would flow into her account.

She adjusted her glasses, which had slipped down to the end of her nose during the dance, and looked out of the window. She could hardly wait to tell Mma. Ramotswe all about it, as she knew that she would approve. Mma. Ramotswe had Mma. Makutsi's real interests at heart—she knew that very well. It would be a relief to her to hear that her employee had come up with such a sound project for her spare time. This was exactly the spirit of enterprise which Mma. Ramotswe had spoken about on a number of occasions. Enterprise with compassion. Those poor men, desperate to know how to type, but too ashamed to ask how to do it, had relief in store.

CHAPTER SEVEN

WHAT MR. MOLEFELO DID

MR. MOLEFELO sat on his rock, under the empty sky, watched by a small herd of cattle that had gathered not far off, and told Mma. Ramotswe, his confessor, of what he had done all those years ago.

"I came to Gaborone when I was eighteen. I had grown up in a small village outside Francistown, where my father was the clerk of the village council. It was an important job in the village, but not important outside. I found out when I came to Gaborone that being a village clerk was nothing and that nobody had heard of him down here.

"I had always been good with my hands, and I had been entered by my school for a place in the Botswana Technical College, which was much smaller then than it is today. I had done well at school in all the science subjects, and I think my father hoped that I would end up designing rockets or something like that. He had no idea that this sort of work is not done in Gaborone; in his eyes, Gaborone was a place where anything could happen.

"My family did not have much money, but I was given a government scholarship to help me in my studies at the college. This was meant to provide you with just enough money to pay the fees and to live simply for the rest of the term. That was not easy, and there were many days when I was hungry. But that does not matter so much when you are young. It is easy to have no money then because you think that it will change and there will be money, and food, tomorrow.

"The college arranged for students to stay with families in Gaborone. These were people who had a spare room, or even in some cases just a shed, which they wanted to rent out. Some of us had to live in uncomfortable places, far from the college. Others were lucky and had rooms in houses where they gave you good food and looked after you like one of the family. I was one of these. I had half a room in a house near the prison, staying with the family of one of the senior officials in the prison service. There were three bedrooms in this house, and I shared one of them with another boy from the college. He was always studying and made no noise. He was also very kind to me, and shared the loaves of bread which he got for nothing from his uncle, who worked in a bakery. He also had an uncle who worked in a butchery, and we got free sausages from him. This boy seemed to get everything free, in fact. His clothes were all free, too—they were given to him by an aunt who worked in a shop which sold clothes.

"The woman of the house was called Mma. Tsolamosese. She was a very fat lady—a bit like yourself, Mma—and she was very kind to us. She used to make sure that my shirts were washed and ironed, because she said that my mother would expect that. 'I am your mother in Gaborone,' she said. 'There is one mother up there in Francistown and one mother down here. The one down here is me.'

"The husband was a very quiet man. He did not like his work, I think, because when she asked him what had happened in the prison that day, he simply shook his head and said: 'Prisons are

full of bad men. They do bad things all day. That is what happens.'
I do not remember him saying much more than that.

"I was very happy living in this house and studying at the college. I was happy, too, because I had found a girlfriend at long last. When I was at home I had tried and tried to find a girl who would talk to me, but there was nobody. Now, when I came to Gaborone, I found that there were many girls who were eager to get to know students at the college because they knew that we would be getting good jobs one day, and if they could get us to marry them, that would mean an easy life for them. I know, I know, Mma., it's not as simple as that, but I think that many of these girls did think that way.

"I met a girl who was hoping to train as a nurse. She had been working very hard at school and had already passed most of the examinations that she would need to get into the nurse training programme. She was very kind to me, and I was very happy that she was my girlfriend. We went together to the dances that they had at the college, and she was always dressed very smartly for these. I was proud that the other boys at the college should see me with this girl.

"Then, Mma., I have to tell you, we were so friendly, this girl and myself, that she found out she was expecting a baby. I was the father, she said. I did not know what to say about this. I think that I just looked at her when she told me. I was shocked, I think, because I was just a student and I could not be a father to a baby just yet.

"I told her that I would not be able to help with this baby and that she should send the baby off to her grandmother, who lived at Molepolole. I think I said that grandmothers were used to looking after such babies. She said that she did not think her grandmother was strong enough to do this, as she had been ill, and all her teeth had fallen out. I said that perhaps there was an aunt who could do this.

"I went back to my room in Mma. Tsolamosese's house and did not sleep that night. The boy I shared the room with asked me what was troubling me, and I told him. He said that this was all my fault and that if I spent more time at my books then I would not get into trouble like that. This did not help me very much, and so I asked him what he would do if he were in my shoes. He said that he had an aunt who worked in a nursery school and that he would give the baby to her, and she would look after it for free.

"I saw my girlfriend the next day and asked her whether she was still expecting a baby. I hoped that she had made some sort of mistake, but she replied that the baby was still there and was growing bigger every day. She would have to tell her mother soon, she said, and her mother would tell her father. When that happened, I should have to look out, she said, as her father would probably come and kill me, or he would get somebody else to do that for him. She said that she thought he had already killed somebody in an argument over cattle, although he did not like to talk about it very much. This did not make me feel any happier. I imagined that I would have to leave the college and try to find work somewhere far away from Gaborone, where this man would not be able to find me.

"My girlfriend was now becoming angry with me. The next time I saw her, she shouted at me and told me that I had let her down. She said that because of me, she would have to try to get rid of the baby before it was born. She said that she knew a woman up in Old Naledi who would do this thing, but that because it was illegal, it would cost one hundred pula, which was a lot of money in those days. I said that I did not have one hundred pula, but I would think about ways of getting it.

"I went home and sat in my room, thinking. I had no idea of how I would get the money to pay for her to get rid of the baby. I had no savings, and I could not ask my father for it. He had no money to spare, and he would just be very cross with me if he knew why I wanted such a large sum. It was while I was thinking of this that I heard Mma. Tsolamosese turn on her radio in the room next door. It was a very fine radio, which had taken them a long time to save for. I suddenly thought: *That is something that is worth at least one hundred pula.*

"You will guess what happened, Mma. Yes. That very night, when everybody had gone to bed, I went into that room and took the radio. I went outside and hid it in the bush near the house, in a place where I knew that nobody would find it. Then I went back to the house and I opened the window in that room, so the next morning it would look as if somebody had managed to force the window and had stolen the radio.

"Everything worked exactly as I had planned it. The next morning, when Mma. Tsolamosese went into the room, she started to shout. Her husband got up and he started to shout, too, which was very unusual for a quiet man like that. 'Those bad men have stolen it. They have taken our radio. Oh! Oh!'

"I pretended to be as shocked as everybody else. When the police came, they asked me if I had heard anything that night, and I lied. I said that I had heard a noise, but that I had thought it was just Rra. Tsolamosese getting up in the middle of the night. The police wrote this down in their book, and then they went away. They told Mma. Tsolamosese that it was very unlikely she would get the radio back. 'These people take them over the border and sell them. It will be far away by now. We are very sorry, Mma.'

"I waited until all the fuss had died down, and then I went out to the place where I had hidden the radio. I was very careful to make sure that nobody saw me, which they did not. I then hid the radio under my coat, and I went off to a place near the railway station where I had heard there were people who would buy things without asking any questions. I sat down under a tree, with the radio on my knee, and waited for something to happen. Sure enough, after only about ten minutes, a man came up to me and said that it was a beautiful radio and that it would be worth at least one hundred and fifty pula, if I ever wanted to sell it. I said that I was happy to sell it, and so he said to me: 'In that case, I will give you one hundred pula, because I can tell that you have stolen this radio and it is more risky for me.'

"I tried to argue, but all the time I was worried that the police would suddenly arrive, and so I sold it to him for one hundred pula. I gave the money to my girlfriend that night, and she just cried and cried when she took it from me. She said, though, that she would see me that weekend, after she had been out to Old Naledi to have the baby got rid of.

"I said that I would see her, but I am sorry to say, Mma., that I did not. We used to meet outside a café in the African Mall. She would wait for me, and then we would go for a walk together and look at the shops. She was waiting for me, as normal, but I stood under a tree, some distance away, and watched. I did not have the courage to go up to her and tell her that I no longer wanted to see her. It would have been a simple thing for me to walk up and talk to her, but I did not do this. I just watched from under the tree. After about half an hour, she went away. I saw her walking off, looking down at the ground, as if she was ashamed.

"She sent a letter to me through one of the other boys, whose sister she knew. She said that I should not send her away after everything that had happened. She said that she was crying for the baby, and that I should not have made her go to the woman in Old Naledi. She said, though, that she forgave me and that she would come to see me at the Tsolamosese's house.

"I sent her a letter through the same boy. In it, I told her that

I was now too busy with my studies to see her again and that she should not come to the house, even to say good-bye. I said that I was sorry she was unhappy, but that once she started to train as a nurse she would be very busy and would forget about me. I told her that there were many other boys, and that she would find one quickly if she looked hard enough.

"I know that she received this letter, as the sister who delivered it told her brother that she had done so. A week or so later, though, she came to the house, while we were sitting down for the dinner which Mma. Tsolamosese had cooked for us. One of the Tsolamosese children looked out of the window and said that there was a girl standing at the gate. Mma. Tsolamosese sent the child out to discover what this girl wanted, and the answer came back that she wanted to see me. I had been looking down at my plate, pretending that this thing had nothing to do with me, but now I had to go out and speak to her. 'Maybe Molefelo is a secret heartbreaker,' said Mma. Tsolamosese as I left the room.

"I was very cross with her for coming, and I think that I raised my voice. She just stood there and cried and said that she still loved me, even though I was being cruel to her. She said that she would not disturb my studies and that she would only expect to see me once a week. She also said that she would try to find ways of paying back the one hundred pula that I had given her.

"I said: 'I don't want your money. I am no longer in love with you because I have found out that you are one of those girls who always nag men and make them feel bad about themselves. Boys have to watch out for girls like you.'

"This made her cry even more, and then she said: 'I will wait for you forever. I will think of you every day, and one day you will come back to me. I will write you a letter and then you will know how much I love you.'

"She reached forward and tried to hold my arm, but I pushed her away and turned to go back into the house. She started to follow me, but I pushed her away again, and this time she left. But all the time that this was happening, the Tsolamosese family was watching from the front window of the house.

"When I came back, they had returned to their seats at the table.

" 'You should not treat girls like that,' said Mma. Tsolamosese. 'I am speaking to you now as your mother in this place. No mother would like to see her son behaving like that.'

"The father looked at me, too. Then he said: 'You are behaving like one of the bad men in the prison. They are always pushing and shoving other people. You be careful, or you may find yourself in that place one day. You just be careful.'

"And their son, who had also been watching, said: 'Yes. One day somebody will come and push you. That could happen.'

"I felt very embarrassed over what had happened, and so I lied. I told them that this girl was trying to get me to help her cheat in her examinations and that I was refusing to do this. They were astonished to hear this, and they said that they were sorry they had misjudged me. 'It is a good thing for Botswana that we have honest people like you,' said the father. 'If everybody were like you, then I would be out of a job. There would be no more need for the Botswana Prisons Department.'

"I sat there and said nothing. I was thinking of how I had stolen from these people, and how I had lied to them. I was thinking of how sad I had made my girlfriend and how I had forced her to get rid of our baby. I was thinking of the baby itself. But I just sat there and said nothing while I ate the food of the people whose kindness I had abused. Only the boy who shared my room seemed to know how I was feeling. He looked at me carefully and then he turned away. I realised then that he knew I had done some very bad things.

"There is not much more to say, Mma. After a few weeks, I forgot all about it. I still thought of the radio from time to time, and felt cold inside when I did so, but I never thought of the girl. Then, when I had finished at the college and I had found a job, I began to be too busy to think much about my past. I was lucky. I did very well in business, and I was able to buy the hotel at a very good price. I found a good wife to marry me, and I had the two fine sons I told you about. There are also three daughters. I have everything I need, but after what happened to me when those men came to my farm, I want to clear up my bad conscience. I want to make good the bad deeds that I did."

Mr. Molefelo stopped talking and looked at Mma. Ramotswe, who had been twisting a long blade of grass around her finger as she listened to him speaking.

"Is that everything, Rra.?" she asked after a while. "Have you told me everything?"

Mr. Molefelo nodded. "I have not hidden anything. That is what happened. I remember it very clearly, and I have told you everything."

Mma. Ramotswe stared at him. He was telling the truth, she knew, because the truth was in his eyes.

"That cannot have been easy to say," she said. "You have been very brave. Most people never tell these stories about themselves. Most people make themselves sound better than they really are."

"There would have been no point doing that," said Mr. Molefelo. "The whole point of talking to you was to tell somebody the truth."

"And now?" she asked. "What do you want to do now?"

Mr. Molefelo frowned. "I want you to help me. That is why I have come to see you."

"But what can I do?" asked Mma. Ramotswe. "I cannot change the past. I cannot take you back all those years."

"Of course not. I did not expect you to be able to do that. I just want you to sort this thing out for me."

"How can I do that? I can't bring back that baby. I can't find that radio. I can't prevent the sadness which that girl felt. All these are things which are long dead and buried. How many years is it? Nearly twenty years? That is a long time."

"I know it is a long time. But it might be possible to do something. I would like to pay the Tsolamosese family back. I would like to give some money to the girl. I would like to sort these things out."

Mma. Ramotswe sighed. "Do you think that money can change things? Do you think that just by giving somebody money, you can undo what you did?"

"No," said Mr. Molefelo. "I d not think that. I am not stupid. I would also like to give them an apology. I would like to apologise and also to give them money."

For a few moments there was silence as Mma. Ramotswe pondered this. What would she do herself, she wondered, in these circumstances? If she had the courage, she would go to the people involved and confess what had happened. Then she would try to make amends. This was what he was doing, except for the fact that he was expecting her to do it for him. An indirect apology of that sort was no apology at all, she thought.

"Don't you think," she began, "don't you think that you are just asking me to do your dirty work—or should I call it your hard work—for you? Don't you think that this means you are not really ready to apologise?"

Mr. Molefelo stared at her. He seemed upset, and she wondered whether she was being too direct. It had been difficult enough for him to talk about this without her now making it worse by effectively accusing him of cowardice. And who was she to accuse anybody of cowardice? How did anybody know how brave he would be?

"I'm sorry," she said, reaching out to touch his arm. "I did not mean to be unkind. I understand how hard this is for you."

There was anguish in his expression as he replied. "All I want you to do, Mma., is to find these people. I do not know where they are. Then, when you have found them, I promise you that I shall be brave. I will go to them and I will speak to them directly."

"That is good," said Mma. Ramotswe. "Nobody could ask more of you."

"But will you help?" asked Mr. Molefelo. "Will you help me by coming with me when I go to see them? I do not know whether I will fail at the last moment if you do not come with me."

"Of course I'll come with you," she said. "I will come with you, and I will be saying to myself: *This a brave man. Only a brave man can look at his past wrongs and then face up to them like this.*"

Mr. Molefelo smiled, his relief quite apparent. "You are a very kind lady, Mma. Ramotswe."

"I don't know about that," said Mma. Ramotswe, rising to her feet and dusting off her dress. "But now it is time for us to walk back. And on the walk back, I shall tell you about a little problem I have. It is all about a boy who killed a hoopoe, and I want to hear from you what you think. You are a man with two boys, and maybe you can give me some advice."

CHAPTER EIGHT

THE TYPEWRITERS, AND A PRAYER MEETING

HENEVER SHE walked past the Botswana Secretarial College, Mma. Makutsi felt a surge of pride. She had spent six months of her life at the college, during which time she had scraped an existence, working part-time as a night waitress in a hotel (a job which she hated) and struggling to stay awake during the day. Her resolve and her persistence had paid off, and she would never forget the strength of the applause at the graduation ceremony when, before the proud eyes of her parents, who had sold a sheep to pay for the journey down to Gaborone, she had crossed the stage to receive her secretarial diploma as the leading graduate of the year. Her life, she suspected, would involve no greater triumph than that.

"Do you see that?" she said to the elder apprentice, whom Mr. J.L.B. Matekoni had instructed to help her in the task of fetching the typewriters. "That motto on the notice board up there? *Be accurate.* That's the motto of the college."

"Yes," said the apprentice. "That's a good motto. You don't want to be inaccurate if you are a typist. Otherwise you have to do everything twice. That would not be good."

Mma. Makutsi looked at him sideways. "A good motto for every walk of life, would you not think?"

The apprentice said nothing, and they continued to walk down the corridor that led to the office.

"All the students here are girls, are they not, Mma.?" asked the apprentice.

"Yes," she said. "There is no reason why that should be. But that is how it was in my day."

"I would like to study here, then," said the apprentice. "That would suit me. I should like to sit in a classroom with all those girls."

Mma. Makutsi smiled. "Some of them would like that, too, I think. The wrong sort of girl."

"There are no wrong sort of girls," countered the apprentice. "All girls have their uses. All girls are welcome."

They had arrived at the office, and Mma. Makutsi was announcing herself to the assistant principal's receptionist.

"Mma. Manapotsi will be pleased to see you, Mma.," said the receptionist, glancing appreciatively at the apprentice, who was smiling at her. "She remembers you well."

Mma. Makutsi was shown into Mma. Manapotsi's office while the apprentice remained outside, perched on the edge of the receptionist's desk. He was amusing her by pressing a finger on a blank sheet of paper and leaving a fingerprint of black grease outlined on the surface.

"My trademark," he said. "If I hold hands with a pretty girl—like you—I leave a trademark! It says: My property! Keep off!"

Inside, Mma. Manapotsi greeted Mma. Makutsi warmly. There were enquiries about her current job, and a delicate question as to the salary she was commanding.

"It sounds very important being an assistant detective and assistant manager," said Mma. Manapotsi. "I hope that they are paying you what you deserve. We like our graduates to be properly rewarded."

"They are paying me as much as they can," said Mma. Makutsi. "Very few people get paid what they really deserve, though, do they? Even the president does not get the salary he deserves, I think. We should pay him more, I think."

"That may be so," said Mma. Manapotsi. "I have always thought that the assistant principals of colleges should get more, too. But we must not complain, must we, Mma.? If everybody complained all the time, then there would be no time for anything else but complaints. We do not complain here at the Botswana Secretarial College. We get on with the job."

"That is what I think, too," said Mma. Makutsi.

The conversation continued in this way for a few minutes. From beyond the door that led into the receptionist's room, there was a murmur of voices and an occasional giggle. At length, they reached the subject of the old typewriters, and Mma. Manapotsi confirmed her offer.

"We can fetch them now," she said. "Your young man out there can carry them for you, if he is not too busy with that girl of mine."

"He is always like that with girls," said Mma. Makutsi. "Every girl he meets. It is a sad thing, but that is the way he is."

"We would not want men to ignore us altogether," said Mma. Manapotsi. "But sometimes it would be better if they ignored us a bit."

They made their way to the storeroom where, amid piles of papers and books, the disused typewriters were stacked.

"They are very old," said Mma. Manapotsi, "but most of them could probably be made to work, or almost work. They will need oiling."

"Plenty of that in the garage," remarked the apprentice, turning a roller experimentally.

"Perhaps," said Mma. Manapotsi. "But remember, these machines are not like cars. They are much more delicate."

They returned to Tlokweng Road Speedy Motors, where Mr. J.L.B. Matekoni had agreed the typewriters could be stored and worked upon until Mma. Makutsi had found a place for the classes to be held. Mma. Ramotswe, who had endorsed the plan in spite of some misgivings about whether there would be enough pupils, offered to pay for the placing of a press advertisement drawing attention to the classes, and also expressed an interest in helping with the restoration of the typewriters.

"Motholeli would like to help, too," she said. "She is very keen on machines, that girl, and she has very nimble fingers."

"This business will be a great success," said Mr. J.L.B. Matekoni. "I have a feeling for businesses. I think that this one will do well."

Mma. Makutsi was buoyed by his prediction. She was awed by the thought that she was about to embark on a venture of her own, and the warm words of her employers encouraged her greatly. "Do you really think so, Rra.?"

"I have no doubt of it," said Mr. J.L.B. Matekoni.

IT WAS, it transpired, a time of mutual support. The No. 1 Ladies' Detective Agency supported Tlokweng Road Speedy Motors, providing secretarial and bookkeeping services in the shape of Mma. Makutsi, who still occasionally helped with the servicing of cars as well. In return, Tlokweng Road Speedy Motors paid most of Mma. Makutsi's salary, thus making it possible for her to serve as assistant detective. For her part, Mma. Ramotswe supported Mr. J.L.B. Matekoni, making his evening meal for him and laundering his overalls and those of the apprentices as well. The apprentices, nurtured and trained by Mr. J.L.B. Matekoni, who was tolerant of their foibles as most employers would not be, repaid in their own way. When it came to the restoration of the typewriters, it was they who did most of the work, giving up a great deal of their spare time over the next two weeks in an effort to coax the old machines into serviceability.

It was in this spirit of mutual assistance that everybody agreed to attend a religious meeting at which the younger apprentice was speaking. He had asked them whether they would care to come and hear him speak, as it would be the first time that he had addressed the entire brotherhood of his church, and it was, he said, a very important occasion for him.

"We shall have to go," said Mr. J.L.B. Matekoni. "I don't think we can refuse."

"You are right," said Mma. Ramotswe. "It is very important to him. It is a bit like a prize-giving. If he were getting a prize, we would have to go."

"These things can go on for many hours," warned Mma. Makutsi. "Don't expect to get away in less than three hours. You must eat a big piece of meat before you go, otherwise you will feel weak."

The meeting took place the following Sunday, in a small church near the diamond-sorting building. Mma. Ramotswe and Mr. J.L.B. Matekoni arrived in good time and had been sitting there, contemplating the ceiling, for at least twenty minutes before Mma. Makutsi arrived.

"Now we are all here," whispered Mr. J.L.B. Matekoni. "Only his brother, Charlie, is not coming."

"He'll be with some girl," said Mma. Makutsi. "That is where he is."

Mma. Ramotswe said nothing. She was watching the congregation coming in, waving discreetly to one or two, and smiling at the children. At last the platform party entered—the minister, dressed in a flowing blue gown, and the choir, also in blue, in whose ranks the apprentice was to be seen, smiling encouragingly at his guests.

There were hymns and prayers, and then the minister rose to speak.

"There are sinners all about us," he warned. "They are wearing ordinary clothes, and they walk and talk like any other person. But their hearts are full of sin, and they are plotting more sin as we sit here."

Mr. J.L.B. Matekoni glanced at Mma. Ramotswe. Was his heart full of sin? Was hers?

"Fortunately we can be saved," continued the minister. "All we have to do is to look into our hearts and see what sins are there. Then we can do something about it."

There were murmurs of agreement from the congregation. One man groaned softly, as if in pain, but it was only sin, thought Mma. Ramotswe. Sin makes one groan. The weight of sin. Its mark. Its stain.

"And those who come into this church," said the minister. "They bring their sins in, too. They bring sins into the midst of God's people. They come straight from Babylon."

Mr. J.L.B. Matekoni, who had been looking at his folded hands as the minister spoke, now looked up and saw that people were staring at him, as well as at Mma. Ramotswe and Mma. Makutsi. He nudged Mma. Ramotswe discreetly.

"Yes," said the minister. "There are strangers here. You are very welcome, but you must declare your sins before God's people. We shall help you. We shall make you strong."

There was now complete silence. Mma. Makutsi looked around anxiously. Surely this was no way to welcome visitors. Usually congregations greeted strangers warmly and clapped when you stood up. This must be a strange religion to which the apprentice had subscribed.

The minister now pointed at Mr. J.L.B. Matekoni. "Speak, my brother," he said. "We are listening."

Mr. J.L.B. Matekoni looked frantically at Mma. Ramotswe. "I. . . ." he began. "I am a sinner. Yes—I suppose. . . ."

Suddenly Mma. Ramotswe stood up. "Oh my!" she called out. "I am the sinner here. I am the one! I have committed so many sins that I cannot count them. They are weighty. They are making me sink. Oh! Oh!"

The minister raised his right arm. "The power of the Lord be upon you, my sister! He will release you from these sins! Tell the sins! Speak their awful name!"

"Oh, they are so numerous," said Mma. Ramotswe. "Oh! I cannot bear these sins. They are making me hot. I am feeling the fire of hell! Oh, the fire of hell is consuming me! I am so hot! Oh!"

She sank back on the pew, fanning herself with the hymn sheet.

"The fires!" she shouted. "The fires are all about me. Take me out!"

Mr. J.L.B. Matekoni felt the dig in his ribs.

"I must take her outside," he said to the congregation at large. "The fire—"

Mma. Makutsi rose to her feet. "I will help you. The poor lady. All those sins. Oh! Oh!"

Once outside, they walked as quickly as they could to Mr. J.L.B. Matekoni's car, which was parked alongside a row of believers' cars, outwardly no different from any of them.

"You are a very good actress," said Mr. J.L.B. Matekoni as they drove away. "I was very embarrassed there. I was having to think of sins."

"Maybe I wasn't acting," said Mma. Ramotswe dryly.

CHAPTER NINE

THE CIVIL SERVICE

MR. MOLEFELO had given Mma. Ramotswe very little information. All she knew about the people for whom she was to look was that Mr. Tsolamosese had been a senior officer at the prison; that the Tsolamosese family had lived in a government house near the old airfield; and that the girlfriend, whose name was Tebogo Bathopi, came from Molepolole and was hoping to train as a nurse. This was not a great deal to go on: much would have happened in the course of twenty years; Tebogo would probably have married and changed her name; Mr. Tsolamosese would surely have retired and the family would have left the house. But it was hard to disappear completely in Botswana, where there were fewer than two million people and where people had a healthy curiosity as to who was who and where people had come from. It was very difficult to be anonymous, even in Gaborone, as there would always be neighbours who would want to know exactly what one was doing and who one's people had been. If you wanted anonymity, you had to leave the country altogether and go somewhere like Johannesburg, where nobody knew, nor cared very much, it would seem.

Tracking down the Tsolamosese family would be relatively

easy, thought Mma. Ramotswe. Even if Mr. Tsolamosese had retired from the prison service, there was bound to be somebody at the prison who would know where he had gone. Prison officials were a close-knit community; they lived cheek by jowl with one another in the prison lines, and their families often intermarried. They had to be protective of one another, as there was always the danger that a released prisoner might try to settle a score, which had happened on one or two occasions, as Mma. Ramotswe had read. In one case, a prisoner who succeeded in escaping hid in the house of a warder, under his bed, and waited for him to go off to sleep before he crawled out and stabbed him through his blankets. It had been a chilling incident, although the warder had survived the attack relatively unscathed, and the prisoner had been rearrested and beaten. Such evil was difficult to contemplate, thought Mma. Ramotswe. How could anybody do that sort of thing to a fellow human being? The answer, of course, was that such people were cold inside. They had no feelings, and it was easy for them to do things like that and worse. God would judge them, she knew, but in the meantime they could do a great deal of damage. Worst of all, these people destroyed trust. You used to be able to trust people, but now you had to be so careful, even in a good country like Botswana. It was unimaginably worse in other places, of course, but even in Botswana you had to hold on to your handbag if you walked out at night, in case a young man with a knife came and took it from you. What could be further from the old Botswana ways of courtesy and respect? What, she wondered, would Obed Ramotswe make of it if he were to come back and see what had happened; her father, who, if he found so much as a one-pula note on the roadway, would hand it over to the police, oblivious to their surprise at his honesty.

Mma. Ramotswe decided to divide her task into two. First she would find the Tsolamosese family and propose the reparation which she had discussed with Mr. Molefelo. Then, that piece of the past set to rest, she would set about the more difficult task of tracing Tebogo. The first step, though, was a telephone call to the prison, and an enquiry as to whether Mr. Tsolamosese still worked there. As she had anticipated, the official answered the telephone had not heard the name. Mma. Ramotswe asked then to speak to the oldest person in the office.

"Why do you want to speak to an old person, Mma.?" she had been asked politely.

"Because they know more, Rra.," she had replied.

There was a silence at the other end of the line. Then, after a few moments of hesitation, the oldest official was fetched.

"I am fifty-eight, Mma.," he said, introducing himself over the line. "Is that old enough for you, or do you want somebody who is eighty or ninety?"

"Fifty-eight is very good, Rra.," she said. "A person who is fifty-eight will know what he is talking about."

This remark was well received. "I shall try to help you, if I can. What is it you wish to know?"

"I would like to know if you remember Mr. Tsolamosese," she said. "He worked in the prison some years ago. Perhaps he is no longer working."

"Ah," said the voice. "I was here when he was working here. He was a very quiet man. He did not say very much, but he did well in the service and was very senior."

"He is no longer working, then?" Mma. Ramotswe pressed.

"No, he is not working. In fact, I am sorry to tell you he is late."

Mma. Ramotswe's heart sank. But perhaps Mma. Tsolamosese was still alive, and Mr. Molefelo would be able to make it up to her.

"He had a heart attack, I think," said the voice. "About eight years ago. He was still here then, but he was very ill and he became late."

"And the widow?" asked Mma. Ramotswe.

"She went away. I don't think anybody here knows anything about her. She must have gone back to her village. You could ask the pensions people, of course. She will be getting her widow's pension if she is still alive. That will mean that they will have her address somewhere. You could try them."

"You have been very kind, Rra.," said Mma. Ramotswe. "I have something to give that lady, and you have helped me to find her. You are very kind."

"It is my job to help," said the voice.

"That is very good."

"Yes," said the voice.

"I hope that you are very happy," said Mma. Ramotswe. "You have been very helpful."

"I am very happy," said the voice. "I shall be retiring next year and I shall be growing sorghum."

"I hope it grows well," said Mma. Ramotswe.

"You are very kind, Mma. Thank you."

They said farewell, and Mma. Ramotswe put down the telephone with a smile. In spite of everything, in spite of all the change, with all the confusion and uncertainty which it brought; in spite of the casual disregard with which people were increasingly treating one another these days, there were still people who spoke to others with the proper courtesy, who treated others, whom they did not know, in the way which was proper according to the standards of the old Botswana morality. And whenever that happened, whenever one encountered such behaviour, one was reminded that all was by no means lost.

Her next task was not a telephone call but a visit. She knew the office which dealt with pensions, and she would call there to find out whether Mma. Tsolamosese was still receiving her pension. If she was, then she would have to try to get the address from them, That might be difficult, but not impossible. There was a tendency in government offices to treat everything as confidential, even if it clearly was not, but Mma. Ramotswe had found that there were usually ways round this.

The government pensions office, when she arrived there shortly after lunchtime, was still shut, but Mma. Ramotswe was happy to wait under the shade of a nearby tree until a tired-looking clerk opened the door and peered outside.

The public office to which she was admitted had that typical look and smell of government offices. The furniture, such as it was, was completely functional—straight-backed chairs and simple two-drawer desks. On the wall at the back there was a picture of His Excellency, the president of the Republic of Botswana, and on the other walls there was a map of Botswana, broken down into administrative districts, a calendar supplied by the *Botswana Gazette,* and a fly-spotted framed picture of cattle gathered round a borehole-fed watering tank.

The clerk behind the desk looked at Mma. Ramotswe in a sleepy way.

"I am looking for the widow of a government pensioner," she said, noting the spoiled collar of the clerk's shirt. He would not go far in the civil service, she thought; civil servants were usually proud of their appearance, and this man was not.

"Name?" he said.

"Mine?"

"Pensioner."

Mma. Ramotswe had written the name on a piece of paper, and she passed it to the clerk. Underneath the name she had written: Prisons Department, and after that the date of Mr. Tsolamosese's death.

The clerk looked at the piece of paper and made his way out of the room into a corridor which Mma. Ramotswe could see was lined with lever-arch files. She watched him walk down the shelves until he stopped, extracted a file, and ruffled through some papers. Then he returned to the desk.

"Yes," he said. "There is a widow of that name. She receives a pension from the Prisons Department."

Mma. Ramotswe smiled. "Thank you, Rra. Could you give me her address? I have something to deliver to her."

The clerk shook his head. "No, I cannot do that. The details of the pensioners are confidential. We could not have the whole world coming in here and finding out where these people live. That is not possible."

Mma. Ramotswe took a deep breath. This was precisely what she had feared would happen, and she knew that she would have to be extremely careful. This clerk was not bright, and people like that could show a remarkable tenacity when it came to rules. Because they could not distinguish between meritorious and unmeritorious requests, they could refuse to budge from the letter of the regulations. And there would be no point in trying to reason with them. The best tactic was to undermine their certainty as to the rule. If they could be persuaded that the rule was otherwise, then it might be possible to get somewhere. But it would be a delicate task.

"But that is not the rule," said Mma. Ramotswe. "I would never tell you your job—a clever man like you does not need to be told by a woman how to do his job—but I think that you have got the rule wrong. The rule says that you must not give the name of a pensioner. It says nothing about the address. That you can tell."

The clerk shook his head. "I do not think you can be right, Mma. I am the one who knows the rules. You are the public."

"Yes, Rra. I am sure that you are very good when it comes to rules. I am sure that this is the case. But sometimes, when one has to know so many rules, one can get them mixed up. You are thinking of rule 25. This rule is really rule 24(b), subsection (i). That is the rule that you are thinking of. That is the rule which says that no names of pensioners must be revealed, but which does not say anything about addresses. The rule which deals with addresses is rule 18, which has now been cancelled."

The clerk shifted on his feet. He felt uneasy now and was not sure what to make of this assertive woman with her rule numbers. Did rules have numbers? Nobody had told him about them, but it was quite possible, he supposed.

"How do you know about these rules?" he asked. "Who told you?"

"Have you not read the *Government Gazette?*" asked Mma. Ramotswe. "The rules are usually printed out in the *Gazette,* for everybody to see. Everybody is allowed to see the rules, as they are there for the protection of the public, Rra. That is important."

The clerk said nothing. He was biting his lip now, and Mma. Ramotswe saw him throw a quick glance over his shoulder.

"Of course," she pressed on, "if you are too junior to deal with these matters, then I would be very happy to deal with a more senior person. Perhaps there is somebody in the back office who is senior enough to understand these rules."

The clerk's eyes narrowed, and Mma. Ramotswe knew at that moment that her judgement had been correct: if he called somebody else, he would lose face.

"I am quite senior enough," he said haughtily. "And what you say about the rules is quite correct. I was just waiting to see if you knew. It is very good that you did. If only more members of the public knew about these rules, then our job would be easier."

"You are doing your job very well, Rra.," sad Mma. Ramotswe.

"I am glad that I found you and not some junior person who would know nothing about the rules."

The clerk nodded sagely. "Yes," he said. "Anyway, this is the address of the woman you mention. Here, I'll write it down for you. It is a small village on the way to Lobatse. Maybe you know it. She is living there."

Mma. Ramotswe took the piece of paper from the clerk and tucked it into the pocket of her dress. Then, having thanked him for his help, she went outside, reflecting on how bureaucracy was very rarely an obstruction, provided that one applied to it the insights of ordinary, everyday psychology, insights with which Mma. Ramotswe, more than many, had always been well endowed.

CHAPTER TEN

THE KALAHARI TYPING SCHOOL FOR MEN
THROWS OPEN ITS DOORS (TO MEN)

LOOKING BACK, as she later would do, on the early days of the Kalahari Typing School for Men, Mma. Makutsi, assistant detective at the No. 1 Ladies' Detective Agency and formerly acting manager of Tlokweng Road Speedy Motors, would marvel at just how easy it was to start the school. If all businesses were as easy, she reflected, then the road to plutocracy would be simple indeed. What made it all so simple and so painless? The answers might form the kernel of a business school essay: a good idea; a niche in the market; low start-up costs; and, what is perhaps most important of all, a willingness to work hard. All of these were present in ample measure in the case of the Kalahari Typing School for Men.

The easiest task—potentially the most difficult—had been the finding of a place to hold the classes. This issue had been quickly resolved by the younger apprentice, who offered to speak to the minister about the possible use of the meeting room attached to his church.

"It is never used during the week," he had said. "The minister is always saying that we must share. This is a chance for us to do just that."

The minister was amenable, under the condition that the religious pamphlets be left in the hall so that those attending the classes might have the chance to be saved.

"There will be many sinners wishing to learn to type," he said. "They will see the pamphlets and some of them will realise what sinners they are."

Mma. Makutsi had readily agreed and had taken the typewriters, most of which were now in basic working order even if not all the keys worked, over to the hall, where they were stored in two padlocked cupboards. There were already tables and chairs in the hall, and these could seat over thirty, although the number of pupils would be limited by the ten typewriters available.

Within a few days, everything was prepared. A small advertisement had been inserted in the *Botswana Daily News*, worded in such a way as to appeal to exactly the audience which Mma. Makutsi had in mind.

Men: do you know that it is very important these days to be able to type? If you cannot type, you will be overtaken. There is no room in the modern world for those who cannot type. You can now learn, in confidential conditions, at the Kalahari Typing School for Men, under the supervision of Mma. Grace Makutsi, Dip. Sec. (magna cum laude) (Bw. Sec. Coll.).

Prospective students were then referred to the telephone number of the No. 1 Ladies' Detective Agency and instructed to ask for the Typing School Department.

On the day of publication, Mma. Makutsi was at work earlier than usual. She had obtained an early copy of the paper from the printers and had read and reread the text of the advertisement. It gave her considerable pleasure to see her name in print. It was the first time that she had ever seen this, and she sat and stared at it for some time, thinking, *That's me, that's my name, in print, in the newspaper, me.*

The first call came half an hour later, and one followed another throughout the day. By four o'clock in the afternoon, there were twenty-two firm bookings for a place in the class; ten would start that week, a further ten would be admitted to the second course some two months later, and two were placed on a waiting list.

Mma. Ramotswe shared Mma. Makutsi's pleasure.

"You were right," she said. "There must be many men who are desperate to learn how to type. It is very sad."

"I told you it would work out," said Mr. J.L.B. Matekoni. "I told you."

THE FIRST class took place on a Wednesday evening. Mma. Ramotswe had given Mma. Makutsi the afternoon off so that she could prepare for the occasion, and Mma. Makutsi had spent some time setting out sheets of paper at each desk and distributing the exercise booklet which she had herself typed out and duplicated. On a makeshift blackboard at one end of the room she had drawn, in chalk, the layout of the keyboard, dissected with wavy lines for the domain of each finger and each thumb. This was the basic knowledge of the typist, the foundation stone of the skill that would send the fingers racing across the keyboard and the keys clattering against the roller.

There had never been any doubt about the pedagogical philosophy which would underpin the efforts of the Kalahari Typing School for Men. This was the same as the philosophy of the Botswana Secretarial College, and it held that every finger must be taught to know its place. There would be no shortcuts; there would be no leeway for sloppy habits. The little finger must *think* q; the thumb must *think* space bar. That is how they had put it at the Botswana Secretarial College, and Mma. Makutsi had never heard the philosophy of typing put so succinctly and so truly.

On the basis of this instinctive positioning of fingers, the students would be taught, by sheer repetition, to bridge the gap between perception of the word to be typed (or its imagination) and the movement of the muscles. That was something that could be acquired only through practice, and through the constant performance of standard exercises. Within a few weeks, if the student had any aptitude at all, words could be typed slowly but accurately, even making allowances for the fact that men have larger, more ungainly fingers.

The class was due to begin at six, which gave time for the students to make their way from their workplaces to the hall. Well before that time, however, they had all assembled, and Mma. Makutsi found herself confronted with ten expectant faces. She looked at her watch, counted the students, and announced that the class would begin.

The hour went very quickly. The students were instructed in the insertion of sheets of paper and in the function of the various keys. Then they were asked to type, in unison, on the command of Mma. Makutsi, the word "hat."

"All together," called out Mma. Makutsi, "h and a and t. Now stop."

A hand went up.

"My h does not work, Mma.," said a puzzled-looking, smartly dressed man. "I pressed it twice, but it has not worked. I have typed 'at.'"

Mma. Makutsi was prepared for this. "Some keys are not in

working order," she said. "This does not matter. You must still press them, because you will find that these keys will work in the office. It does not matter at this stage."

She looked at the man, who had his hair parted down the middle and a neatly trimmed moustache. He was smiling up at her, his lips parted slightly, as if he was about to say something. But he did not, and they moved on to new but equally unchallenging words.

"Cat," shouted Mma. Makutsi. "And mat. Hat cat mat."

At the end of the hour, Mma. Makutsi made her way round the desks and inspected the results. She had learned at the Botswana Secretarial College the importance of encouragement, and she made sure that she had a word of praise for each student.

"You will be a very good typist, Rra.," she would say. "You have good finger control." Or: "You have typed 'mat' very clearly. That is very good."

Once the class was over, the men made their way out of the hall, talking enthusiastically amongst themselves. Mma. Makutsi, tidying up in the background, overheard a remark which one of the students passed to another.

"She is a good teacher, that woman," he said. "She does not make me feel stupid. She is good at her job."

Alone in the hall, she smiled to herself. She had enjoyed the class and had discovered a new talent: an ability to teach. And what was more, she had in the small cash box on her desk the first week's fees, in carefully counted notes of the Bank of Botswana. It was a comfortable sum, and there were virtually no overheads to pay. This money was hers to dispose of, although she planned to give a small portion of it to Mma. Ramotswe to cover the cost of the telephone and as a recognition of her contribution to the business. Once she had done that, she would put the balance in her savings account. The days of poverty were over.

After she had locked up, she tucked the cash box into her bag of papers and started the walk back home. She walked along an untarred back road, past small houses from which light spilled, and in which she witnessed, framed in the windows, scenes of everyday domesticity. Children sat at tables, some upright, attentive, while others stared up at the ceiling; parents ladled the evening meal into their bowls; bare lightbulbs in some rooms, coloured lamp shades in others; music drifted from kitchens, a young girl sat on the kitchen step, singing a snatch of song which Mma. Makutsi remembered from her own childhood, and which made her stop for a moment, there in the shadows, and remember.

CHAPTER ELEVEN

MMA. RAMOTSWE GOES TO A SMALL VILLAGE TO THE SOUTH OF GABORONE

SHE DROVE down in the tiny white van, the morning sun streaming through the open window, the air warm against her skin, the grey-green trees, the browning grass, the plains stretching out on both sides of the road. The traffic was light; an occasional van, minibuses crowded and swaying on their ruined suspension, a truck full of green-uniformed soldiers, the men calling out to any girl walking along the edge of the road, private cars speeding down to Lobatse and beyond on their unknown business. Mma. Ramotswe liked the Lobatse road. Many trips in Botswana were daunting in their length, particularly the trip up to Francistown, in the north, which seemed to go on forever, along a straight ribbon of a road. Lobatse, by contrast, was little more than an hour away, and there was always just enough activity on the way to keep boredom at bay.

Roads, thought Mma. Ramotswe, were a country's showcase. How people behaved on roads told you everything you needed to know about the national character. So the Swazi roads, on which she had driven on one frightening occasion some years earlier, were fraught with danger, full of those who overtook on the wrong side and those who had a complete disregard for speed limits. Even the Swazi cattle were more foolhardy than Botswana cattle. They seemed to lurch in front of cars as if inviting collision, challenging drivers at the very last moment. All of this was because the Swazis were an ebullient, devil-may-care people. That was how they were, and that was how they drove. Batswana were more careful; they did not boast, as the Swazis tended to do, and they drove more carefully.

Of course, cattle were always a problem on the roads, even in Botswana, and there was nobody in Botswana who did not know somebody, or know of somebody who knew somebody, who had collided with a cow. This could be disastrous, and each year people were killed by cattle which were knocked into the car itself, sometimes impaling drivers on their horns. It was for this reason that Mma. Ramotswe did not like to drive at night, if she could possibly avoid it, and when she had to do so, she crawled along, peering into the darkness ahead, ready to brake sharply if the black shape of a cow or a bull should suddenly emerge from the darkness.

A journey was a good time to think, and as she drove, Mma. Ramotswe mulled over in her mind the possible outcomes of this rather unusual affair. The more she thought about Mr. Molefelo, the more she admired what he had done in coming to see her. Most do not bother with the really old wrongs; many forget them entirely, whether deliberately—if you can make a deliberate effort to forget—or by allowing the past to fade of its own accord. Mma. Ramotswe wondered whether people have a duty to keep memories alive, and had decided that they have. Certainly the old beliefs were that those who had gone before should be remembered. There were rituals to this effect, the purpose of which was to remind you of your duties to grandparents and great-grandparents, and the parents of grandparents and their parents, too. If you did not remember them, then they might pine and die, not here, of course, but in those other places where the ancestors lived; somewhere over there, where you could not see. Half of Botswana thought that way, and the other half thought the church way, which held that when you died you went to heaven, if you deserved it, of course, and once you were there you were looked after by saints and angels and people like that. Some people said that there were cattle in heaven, too, which was probably true; white cattle, with sweet breath, and watery brown eyes; saintly cattle who moved slowly and allowed children, the late children, to ride on their backs. What fun for those poor children, who had never known their mothers and fathers perhaps, because they had died too young; what a consolation that they should have these gentle cattle to be their companions. Mma. Ramotswe thought this, and then, for a moment, she felt tears well in her eyes. She had lost her baby, and where was she? She hoped that her baby was happy and would be waiting for her when she herself left Botswana and went to heaven. Would Mr. J.L.B. Matekoni get round to naming a wedding date before then? She hoped so, although he certainly seemed to be taking his time. Perhaps they could get married in heaven, if he left it too late. That would certainly be cheaper.

To return to Mr. Molefelo and Mma. Tsolamosese. It was difficult to anticipate what Mma. Tsolamosese would say when the truth was revealed to her about what had happened all those years ago. She would be angry, no doubt, and she might even talk of going to the police. Mr. Molefelo had presumably not thought of that possibility when he came to her with the request to trace Mma. Tsolamosese. He had assumed that the matter could be cleared up informally, but if Mma. Tsolamosese made a complaint at the local police station, then they might feel obliged to press charges. It would be surprising if they did that, after all those years, but Mma. Ramotswe imagined that there was nothing in the Botswana Penal

Code to prevent that happening. She had not read the Botswana Penal Code from cover to cover; in fact she had not read it at all, but it could be bought from the Government Printer for a few pula; she had seen copies lying about and had paged through one of these, but it had not been immediately obvious to her what the Code was trying to say. This was the difficulty with laws and with legal language: they used language which very few people, apart from lawyers, understood. Penal Codes, then, were all very well, but she wondered whether it might not be simpler to rely on something like the Ten Commandments, which, with a bit of modernisation, seemed to give a perfectly good set of guidelines for the conduct of one's life, or so Mma. Ramotswe thought. Everybody knew that it was particularly wrong to kill; everybody knew that it was wrong to steal; everybody knew that it was wrong to commit adultery and to covet one's neighbour's goods . . . She hesitated. No they did not. They did not know that at all, or at least not anymore. There were children, horrible, cheeky children being brought up with precisely the opposite message ringing in their ears, and that was the problem, she thought grimly. People were far too ready to abandon their husbands and wives because they had tired of them. If you woke up one day and thought that you might find somebody more exciting than the person you had, then you could walk out! Just like that! And you could take it even further, could you not, and just walk out on all sorts of people. If you decide that your parents are beginning to bore you, then just walk out! And friends, too. They could become very demanding, but all you had to do was to walk out. Where had all this come from, she wondered. It was not African, she thought, and it certainly had nothing to do with the old Botswana morality. So it must have come from somewhere else.

To return to Mr. Molefelo and Mma. Tsolamosese once again. Mma. Ramotswe hoped that Mma. Tsolamosese would not be inclined to go to the police, to rake over these very old coals; in which case she would inform her that Mr. Molefelo wished to make an apology and buy her a new radio. She had not discussed with him the precise terms of his amends, but he had said to her that money would be no object. "I shall pay whatever it takes," he had said. "My conscience is more important to me than money. You can get lots of money out of the bank. You cannot get peace of mind out of the bank."

Well, she would have to see what happened and handle matters accordingly. It would not be long now, with the turning to the village coming up, badly signposted, and a bumpy track to be negotiated up the hillside to Mma. Tsolamosese's house, which, if her directions were correct, she could just make out at the edge of the village.

An elderly woman was sitting on a stool outside the house, pounding corn in a traditional wooden mortar. She stopped as the tiny white van drew up, and rose to her feet to greet Mma. Ramotswe.

They exchanged greetings in the traditional way.

"Dumela, Mma.," Mma. Ramotswe said. "Have you slept well?"

"Yes, Mma. I have slept well."

Mma. Ramotswe introduced herself and asked whether the woman was Mma. Tsolamosese.

The woman smiled. She had a pleasant, open expression, and Mma. Ramotswe warmed to her immediately. "I am Mma. Tsolamosese. This is my place."

Mma. Ramotswe accepted the invitation to sit down on a wooden chair, strung with strips of leather. It was not strong-looking, but she knew that these traditional chairs were well made and could bear her weight. The woman then went inside and fetched a mug of water for her visitor, which Mma. Ramotswe accepted gratefully.

The house was of average size for such a village. It was square, neatly thatched, and had mud-daub walls of a warm ochre colour. The front door was painted white but had been scratched at the base by a dog. From inside the house, which was dark, as the curtains were drawn, there came the sound of two childish voices.

"There are two children who live here," said Mma. Tsolamosese. "There is the daughter of one of my sons, whose wife has gone to look after her mother in Shashe. Then there is the daughter of my daughter, who is late. I am looking after both of these children."

"That is the work of so many women," said Mma. Ramotswe. "Children and more children, all the time until we die. That seems to be what women have to do."

Mma. Tsolamosese nodded her agreement. She was looking very carefully at Mma. Ramotswe, her intelligent gaze moving over her visitor's face and clothes, going off to the tiny white van and then back.

"I have looked after children all my life," said Mma. Tsolamosese. "It started when I was fourteen and had to look after my older sister's child. Then it carried on when I had my own children, and now I am a grandmother and the task is not finished." She paused for a moment and then continued: "Why have you come to see me, Mma.? I am very happy to see you, but I wonder why you have come."

Mma. Ramotswe laughed. "I have not come all this way to discuss children with you," she said. "I have come to talk to you about something which happened a long time ago."

Mma. Tsolamosese opened her mouth to say something, but stopped. She was puzzled, and eager to find out, but she would wait for her visitor to explain herself.

"I believe your late husband worked for the Prison Department," Mma. Ramotswe said.

"He did," said Mma. Tsolamosese. "He was a good man. He worked for the department for many years and was quite senior. Thanks to that, I get a pension today."

"And you lived near the old airfield in Gaborone?" went on Mma. Ramotswe. "And you let students live in your spare room?"

"We always did that," said Mma. Tsolamosese. "It helped with housekeeping money. Not that they could pay much rent."

"There was a student called Molefelo," said Mma. Ramotswe. "He was studying at the Botswana Technical College. Do you remember him?"

Mma. Tsolamosese smiled. "I remember that boy well. He was a very nice boy. He was always clean."

Mma. Ramotswe hesitated. It was not going to be easy to tell her; even now, at this distance in time, it would be news of a gross betrayal. But she had to do it; it was part of her job to be the bearer of bad news, and she would have to steel herself.

"When he was staying with you," she said, watching Mma. Tsolamosese's face closely, "you had a burglary. A man forced a window and stole a radio. Did that happen?"

Mma. Tsolamosese frowned. "Yes, it did happen. I would not forget a thing like that. It was a very fine radio."

Mma. Ramotswe drew a deep breath. She would have to do it. "Molefelo took it," she said. "He stole the radio."

At first, Mma. Tsolamosese looked confused. Then she reached down and dipped her fingers into the maize flour in the mortar.

"No," she said. "He did not do it. He was living with us when it happened. You have got it wrong. Somebody else stole it. One of the prisoners, I think. That is always a danger when you live near a prison."

"No, Mma.," said Mma. Ramotswe, her voice gentle. "It was not a prisoner. It was Molefelo. He needed money urgently for some . . . something he had to do. So he stole your radio and made it look like a burglary. He sold it for one hundred pula to a man near the railway station. That is what happened."

Mma. Tsolamosese looked up sharply. "How do you know this, Mma.? How can you talk about this thing if you weren't even there?"

Mma. Ramotswe sighed. "He told me himself. Molefelo. He is feeling very bad—he has felt bad about it for years—and now he wants to come and apologise. He wants to buy you a new radio. He wants to make it up."

"I do not want a radio," said Mma. Tsolamosese. "I do not like the music they play all the time now. Clank, clank. They do not play good music anymore."

"It is important to him," said Mma. Ramotswe. She paused. "Have you ever done anything bad yourself, Mma.?"

Mma. Tsolamosese stared at her. "Everybody has," she said.

"Yes," said Mma. Ramotswe. "Everybody has. But do you ever remember wanting to set right some bad thing you have done? Do you remember that at all?"

There was a silence between them. Mma. Tsolamosese looked away, out across the hillside. Seated on her stool, she was now hugging her knees. When she spoke, her voice was quiet.

"Yes, I do. I remember that."

Mma. Ramotswe lost no time. "Well, that is how Molefelo feels. And should you not give him the chance to say sorry?"

The reply was not immediate, but it did come. "Yes," she said. "It was a long time ago. It is good that he is thinking this now. I would not want him to suffer in his heart."

"You are right, Mma.," said Mma. Ramotswe. "What you are doing is the right thing."

They sat together in the sunlight. There were beans to be shelled, and Mma. Ramotswe did this while Mma. Tsolamosese continued to crush maize, a gnarled hand on the pestle, the other on the rim of the wooden mortar. They had drunk a mug of heavily sweetened tea and felt relaxed and comfortable in one another's company. Mma. Tsolamosese was now quite happy about the apology, and had agreed that Mma. Ramotswe should bring Molefelo out so that they could meet.

"He was just a young boy then," said Mma. Tsolamosese. "What he did then is nothing to do with the man he has become."

"Yes," said Mma. Ramotswe. "He is a different person."

A young teenage girl, barefoot and wearing a shabby green dress, appeared at the door and bobbed politely to Mma. Ramotswe.

"This is the daughter of my son," said Mma. Tsolamosese. "She is very helpful with the little one. Bring her out to see, Koketso. Bring her out to see Mma."

The girl went back into the house and came out carrying a toddler of two. She placed the child on its legs and held its hand while it took a few tentative steps.

"This is the child of my late daughter," said Mma. Tsolamosese. "I am looking after her, as I told you."

Mma. Ramotswe reached across and took the child's hand in her own.

"She is a very pretty child, Mma.," she said. "She will grow into a very pretty lady in time."

Mma. Tsolamosese looked at her and turned her head away. Mma. Ramotswe thought that she had offended her in some way but could not work out why this should be. It was perfectly polite to compliment a grandmother on the prettiness of her granddaughter; indeed, not to do so would have been unfeeling.

"Take her off now, Koketso," said Mma. Tsolamosese. "I

think that she might be hungry. There is some pap near the stove. You can give that to her."

The teenage girl came forward to pick up the child and retreated into the house. Mma. Ramotswe continued with her shelling of the beans but sneaked a glance at Mma. Tsolamosese, who had renewed her pounding of the maize.

"I'm sorry if I upset you," said Mma. Ramotswe. "I did not mean to."

Mma. Tsolamosese put down her pestle. Her voice, when she spoke, sounded tired: "It is not your fault, Mma. You were not to know. That child . . . the mother, who is late, had that disease which has run this way and that way through the country, and everywhere. That is what took her. And the child. . . ."

Mma. Ramotswe could tell what was coming.

"The doctor said that the child will become ill, too, sooner or later," said Mma. Tsolamosese. "She will not live. That is why I was upset. You did not mean it, but you were talking about something that will never be."

Mma. Ramotswe pushed aside her half-filled bowl of shelled beans and went over to Mma. Tsolamosese's side, putting an arm about her shoulder.

"I am sorry, Mma.," she said. "I am so sorry, sorry."

There was nothing more that could be said, but as she stood there, sharing the moments of private grief, the idea had come to her of what Mr. Molefelo could do.

CHAPTER TWELVE

THE MIRACLE THAT WAS WROUGHT AT
TLOKWENG ROAD SPEEDY MOTORS

THE STUDENTS of the Kalahari Typing School for Men met at
the church hall every weekday night, with the exception of Fri-
days. Their progress was rapid; indeed Mma. Makutsi had to
revise her estimates of how long it would take them to become
proficient typists and was able to announce to them that the
course would last five weeks, rather than six.

"You will get the same diploma," she announced, making a
mental note to do something about the printing of the certifi-
cates. "It will be the same course, but you people will have finished it one week early."

"Will we get some money back?" asked one of the men, causing a ripple of laughter amongst the others.

"No," said Mma. Makutsi. "Certainly not. You will get the
same amount of knowledge. So that costs the same amount. That
is only fair."

They appeared to accept this without complaint, and she
moved on, with relief, to the next assignment. To give them a
change from copy typing, they were all invited to compose a short
essay in the remaining half hour of the class. They would need to
produce only half a page at the most, but they should try to do

this with as few mistakes as possible. There would be fifty marks for a perfect essay, with two marks being subtracted for each mistake. The topic, she announced, was to be "The Important Things in My Life" and the essay should be written anonymously and claimed back later. This would avoid embarrassment: people could write about what really mattered to them without feeling awkward. The title was not an original idea; at school she herself had written a prizewinning essay on the subject, and it had remained with her as the perfect essay topic. Nobody would be stuck for something to say: everybody had something in which they were interested.

The students set to the essay with vigour. At the end of the class, the essays were all left on the table and collected by Mma. Makutsi. She intended to take them home and read them there, but a glance at the topmost essay so absorbed her that she sat down and read through them all. All of life seemed to be laid out before her: mothers, wives, football teams, ambitions at work, cherished motor cars; everything that men liked.

This one was typical: "There are so many things that are important to me in my life. I find it difficult to chose which things are the most important, but I think that the Zebras Football Team is one of them. Ever since I was a little boy I wanted to play for the Zebras, but I was never much good at football. So I watched from the stands and shouted very loudly for the Zebras to win. When that happens, I feel very happy and I spend the night celebrating with my friends, who are also Zebra fans. I cannot imagine Botswana without the Zebras. It would not be the same country, and we would all feel that something was missing from our lives."

This was almost perfectly typed, and Mma. Makutsi was impressed with the clarity of expression. "The reader," she wrote in the margin, "is left in no doubt of the importance of the Zebras in your life." She paged through another couple of essays; there was another hymn of praise to the Zebras and a touching tribute to a young son and his doings. Then, almost at the bottom of the heap, she found: "I have discovered something very important in my life. I did not expect to find it, but it came to me suddenly, like lightning. I am not a man who has had much excitement in his life, but this thing is very exciting and my heart has been racing for more than one week. It is a lady I have met. She is one of the most beautiful ladies I have ever seen, and I think that she must be one of the kindest, nicest ladies in Botswana. She always smiles at me and does not mind if I make mistakes. She has walked past me, and has made my heart sing, although she does not know it. I do not know whether to tell her that she is filling my head with ideas of love. If I tell her, she might say that I am not good enough for her. But if I do not tell her, then she may never know how I feel. She is the most important thing in my life. I cannot stop thinking of her, even when she is teaching me typing."

Mma. Makutsi stood stock-still, as anybody would do on coming across so unambiguous a declaration of love. One of her students, one of these men, was in love with her! She thought that nobody could fall in love with her, and one of these men had done just that. Oh! Oh!

She looked at the essay. Of course, there was no name on it, but there was no doubt about the author. She had been so engrossed in the sense that she had paid little attention to the typing. Every letter h was missing. "S e is t e most important t ing in my life," the essay read. "I cannot stop t inking of er."

Her heart beating with excitement, she took out a pencil and wrote at the bottom of the essay: "This is a very moving essay, which is well typed. You should tell this lady, though, or she might never know. You should ask her to go out with you after the class. That is what you should do."

THAT AFTERNOON, Tlokweng Road Speedy Motors had been left in the hands of the two apprentices. Both Mr. J.L.B. Matekoni and Mma. Ramotswe had gone out to the orphan farm to fix a pump—in the case of Mr. J.L.B. Matekoni—and to talk to the matron, Mma. Silvia Potokwani—in the case of Mma. Ramotswe. Mma. Makutsi, who was allowed three afternoons off a month, had decided that afternoon to go downtown to deposit money in her savings account, which had grown considerably with the income from the typing school, and to purchase a new pair of shoes. Her current pair, with their bright red buttons, would be left for resoling, and she had her eye on a new pair which she had spotted in the window of a shop in the town. The shoes themselves were light green, with lowish heels (which were very important for comfort and walking; high heels were always a temptation, but, like all temptations, one paid for them later). On each toe there was a large leather bow, also in green, and the linings were sky blue. It was the sky-blue linings that particularly appealed to her, and she imagined the pleasure that would come from putting one's feet into such surroundings each morning. They were rather more expensive than her normal shoes, but such footwear could not be expected to come cheaply, especially with linings like that. She had seen them and known immediately that they must be hers. With these green shoes, the good fortune which had entered her life with the successful setting up of the Kalahari Typing School for Men would surely continue. They were also shoes that would give the wearer confidence: a person could speak with authority in such shoes.

The apprentices enjoyed being left by themselves. They assured Mr. J.L.B. Matekoni that they would not give any repair estimates, although it was agreed that they could get on with existing work. There was a troublesome mud-coloured French station wagon parked in front of the garage, and they would work on that, trying to fix two doors that would not shut properly and to deal with an overheating engine. They were familiar with the car, which they had tried to fix before on at least two occasions, and its problems were something of a personal challenge to them.

"That French car will keep you busy," said Mr. J.L.B. Matekoni. "But be careful with it. That car is a liar."

"A liar, Rra.?" asked the younger apprentice. "How can a car be a liar?"

"Its instruments do not tell the truth," said Mr. J.L.B. Matekoni. "You can adjust them, but they go back to their old ways. A car that does that is a liar. You can do very little about it."

Left to themselves, the apprentices made a cup of tea and sat on their oil drums for half an hour. Charlie, the older apprentice, called out to any girls who were passing, shouting out invitations to come and see inside the garage.

"Lots going on in this garage," he called out. "Come on. Come and take a look. There's lots for a girl like you to do in here!"

The younger apprentice tried to look the other way as the girls went past, but usually failed, sneaking a glance, but not calling out. After they had finished their tea, they drove the mud-coloured French station wagon onto the new hydraulic ramp which Mr. J.L.B. Matekoni had recently had installed. This was the first disobedience, the apple in Eden, as they had been given strict instructions that the only person to operate this was Mr. J.L.B. Matekoni himself. But now, faced with the chance to elevate the French car, they could not resist.

The ramp worked magnificently, lifting the car with consummate ease. But then it stopped, the extended central steel piston shining with oil, the car perched precariously above the mechanism. The older apprentice pushed the deflation switch, but nothing happened. He tried again and then turned the power on and off. Nothing happened.

"Broken," said the younger apprentice. "Your fault."

They sat down on their oil drums and stared miserably at the elevated car.

"What is Mr. J.L.B. Matekoni going to say?" said the younger apprentice.

"I'm going to say that we had nothing to do with it," said the older apprentice. "I'm going to say it was an accident. We parked the car above the ramp and then it went off by itself. We didn't touch it."

The younger apprentice looked at him. "I cannot tell lies anymore," he said. "Now that I am saved, I cannot lie."

The older one met his stare. "Then you will get both of us into bad trouble. Really bad trouble." He paused. "So I'm going to say that you did it. I'll tell him that it was you."

"You would not do that to me," said the younger apprentice. "And anyway, I would tell him the truth. The boss can tell when somebody is lying. Mma. Ramotswe can, too. You would never be able to fool her." He paused. "But there is something we can do."

"Oh yes," said the older apprentice, mocking him. "Pray?"

"Yes," the younger one said as he slid off the oil drum and went down on his knees. "Oh Lord," he said. "Release this car," adding, "please."

There was silence. Outside, a large truck went past, grinding its gears. A cicada began to screech in the scrub bush at the back; a grey dove fluttered its wings briefly in the bough of the acacia tree beside the garage. And there was heat over the land.

Suddenly there was a hissing sound. They looked up, both surprised. The trapped air in the hydraulic system was clearing, allowing the column and its burden to descend gracefully towards the ground.

CHAPTER THIRTEEN

TEA AT THE ORPHAN FARM

MMA. SILVIA Potokwani was the matron of the orphan farm, which lay twenty minutes' drive to the east of the town. She had worked there for fifteen years, as deputy matron and then as matron, and it was said that she remembered the name of every orphan who had passed through her hands. This was never put to the test, but if one of the staff ever asked her: "I was trying to remember the name of that boy who came from Maun, the one with the sticking-out ears who was such a quick runner, can you remind me, Mma.?" she would reply, without hesitation, "Cedric Motoposipe. He had a brother who was no good at athletics but became a very good cook and is now working at the Sun Hotel as a chef. Good boys, both of them." Or somebody might ask: "That girl who went to live in Lobatse when she left us and married a policeman, what was her name?" and Mma. Potokwani would reply: "Memedi Gafetsili."

Not only did Mma. Potokwani remember the names of all the orphans, but she also knew anybody of any consequence in Botswana. Once she met anybody, she filed away their details in her mind and, in particular, she remembered in what way they might help the orphan farm; those who had money would be asked for donations; butchers would be asked for spare offcuts; bakers would be asked for surplus doughnuts and cakes. These requests were rarely refused; it would take a degree of courage that few possessed to turn Mma. Potokwani down, and as a result the orphans very seldom wanted for anything.

Mr. J.L.B. Matekoni, who had known Mma. Potokwani for over twenty years, was called out regularly to deal with any mechanical problems which arose. He kept alive the old van which they used to transport orphans—this involved much scouring of the country for spare parts, as the van was an old one—and he also attended to the borehole pump, which lost a certain amount of oil and tended to overheat. It would have been possible to recommend that their old machinery, including this pump, be scrapped, but he knew that Mma. Potokwani would never accede to such a suggestion. She believed in getting as much use as possible from everything, and thought that as long as machinery, or anything else, could be cajoled into operation, it should be kept; to do otherwise, she thought, was wasteful. Indeed, the last time that Mma. Ramotswe had drunk tea with her in the office at the orphan farm, she had noticed that her china cup had been repaired several times, once on the handle and twice elsewhere.

Now, parking Mr. J.L.B. Matekoni's truck in a place under an old frangipani tree specially reserved for visitors, they saw Mma. Potokwani waving to them out of her window. By the time they had alighted from the truck and Mr. J.L.B. Matekoni had taken out the tool kit that he would need to repair the pump, Mma. Potokwani had emerged from the front door of the office and was advancing towards them.

She greeted them warmly. "My two very good friends," she said, "both arriving at the same time! Mma. Ramotswe and her fiancé, Mr. J.L.B. Matekoni!"

"He is my driver now," joked Mma. Ramotswe. "I do not have to drive anymore."

"And I do not have to cook anymore," added Mr. J.L.B. Matekoni.

"But you never did cook, Rra.," said Mma. Potokwani. "What is this talk about cooking?"

"I sometimes cooked," said Mr. J.L.B. Matekoni.

"When did you cook?" asked Mma. Potokwani.

"Sometimes," said Mr. J.L.B. Matekoni. "But we must not stand around and talk about cooking. I must go and fix this pump of yours. What is it doing now?"

"It is making a very strange noise," said Mma. Potokwani. "It is unlike the other times when it has made a strange noise. This time it sounds like an elephant when it trumpets. That is the sort of noise it makes. Not all the time, but every now and then. It is also shaking like a dog. That is what it is doing."

Mr. J.L.B. Matekoni shook his head. "It is a very old pump," he said. "Machinery doesn't last forever, you know. It is just like us. It has to die sometime."

He could tell that Mma. Potokwani was not prepared to entertain such defeatist talk.

"It may be old," she said, "but it is still working, isn't it? If I have to go out and buy a new pump, then that will take money which could be used for other things. The children need shoes. They need clothes. I have to pay the housemothers and the cooks and everybody. There is no money for new pumps."

"I was just pointing out the truth about machines," said Mr. J.L.B. Matekoni. "I did not say I would not try to fix it."

"Good," said Mma. Potokwani, bringing the pump discussion to a close. "We are all fond of that pump. We do not want it to go just yet. One day, maybe, but not yet."

She turned to Mma. Ramotswe. "While Mr. J.L.B. Matekoni

is fixing the pump," she said, "we shall go and have tea. Then, when he has finished, his tea will be ready. I have also made a fruitcake, and there will be a very big piece set aside for him."

THE PUMP house was at the other end of a wide field that bordered the row of cottages in which the orphans lived. There was a large vegetable patch at the side of this field, and then the field itself, which had been used for maize and which was still covered by the withered stalks of the last year's crop. The borehole which the pump served was a good one, tapping into an underground stream which was fed, Mr. J.L.B. Matekoni suspected, by waters that seeped down from the dam. He had always found it surprising that there should be so much underground water in a dry country; that underneath these great brown plains, which could get so parched in the dry season, there could still be deep lakes of sweet, fresh water. Of course you could not rely on there being water underground. When they had built the big stone house out at Mokolodi, they had found it very difficult to get any water at all. They had consulted the best water diviners there were, and these men had walked this way and that with their sticks in their hands, and nothing had happened; there had simply been no movement. For some reason, the underground water was not there. Eventually they had been obliged to use an old water tanker to bring water for the house.

Mr. J.L.B. Matekoni walked across the field, the dust on his shoes, the dried mealie stalks cracking under his feet. The earth was generous, he thought: sand and soil could be persuaded, with a little water, to yield such life, and to make such good things for the table. Everything depended on that simple generosity: trees, cattle, pumpkin vines, people—everything. And this soil, the soil on which he walked, was special soil. It was Botswana. It was his soil. It had made the very bodies of his people; of his father, Mr. P. Z. Matekoni, and his grandfather, Mr. T. Matekoni, before him. All of them, down the generations, were linked by this bond with this particular part of Africa, which they loved, and cherished, and which gave them so much in return.

He looked up. Mr. J.L.B. Matekoni always wore a hat when he was outside; a brown hat with no hatband, made of thin felt of some description, and very old, like the orphan-farm pump. He tilted his hat back slightly, so that he could see the sky more clearly. It was so empty, so dizzying in its height, so unconcerned by the man who was crossing a field beneath it, and thinking as he did so.

He walked on and reached the pump house. The pump, which was controlled by an automatic switch attached to the water storage tank, was in action as he reached it. It sounded as if it was working normally, and Mr. J.L.B. Matekoni wondered whether Mma. Potokwani had been imagining the problem. But even as he stood there, before the pump house door, thinking of the large slice of fruitcake to which he could now return, the pump issued the strange sound which Mma. Potokwani had described. It did indeed sound like the trumpeting of an elephant, but to Mr. J.L.B. Matekoni's ears it meant something much more worrying: it was the pump's death rattle.

He sighed and entered the pump house, taking care to look out for snakes, which liked to lie in such places. He reached out and flicked the manual override switch. The pump groaned and then stopped. Now there was silence, and Mr. J.L.B. Matekoni put down his toolbox and extracted a spanner. He felt weary. Life was a battle against wear; the wear of machinery and the wear of the soul. Oil. Grease. Wear.

He laid down his spanner. No. He would not fix this pump anymore. Mma. Potokwani was always telling him to do this and do that, and he had always done it. How many times had he fixed this pump? At least twenty times, probably more. And he had never charged a single thebe for his time, and of course he never would. But there came a time when one had to stand up to somebody like Mma. Potokwani. She had been so kind to him when he was ill—although now he remembered so little of that strange time of confusion and sadness—and he would always be loyal to her. But he was the mechanic, not she. He was the one who knew when a pump had come to the end of its life and needed to be replaced. She knew nothing about pumps and cars, although sometimes she behaved as if she did. She would have to listen to him for a change. He would say: "Mma. Potokwani, I have examined the pump, and it can no longer be fixed. It is broken beyond all repair. You must telephone one of your donors and tell them that a new pump is needed."

He closed the door behind him, taking one last look at the pump. It was an old friend, in a way. No modern pump would look like that, with its wheel and its beautiful heavy casing; no modern pump would make a noise like the trumpeting of an elephant. This pump had come from far away and could be given back to the British now. *Here is your pump, which you left in Africa. It is finished now.*

"SUCH GOOD cake," said Mma. Ramotswe, accepting the second slice which Mma. Potokwani had placed on her plate. "These days I find I do not have the time for baking. I should like to make cakes, but where is the time?"

"This cake," said Mma. Potokwani, licking crumbs off her fingers, "is made by one of the housemothers who is a very good cook, Mma. Gotofede. Whenever I am expecting visitors, she makes a cake. And all the time she is looking after the children in her cottage. And you know how much work that entails."

"They are good women, these housemothers," said Mma. Ramotswe, looking out of the window to where a couple of the women were enjoying a break from their labours, chatting on the verandah of one of the neat cottages in which groups of ten or twelve orphans lived.

Mma. Potokwani followed her gaze. "That is Mma. Gotofede over there," she said. "The lady with the green apron. She is the one who is such a good cook."

"I knew somebody of that name once," said Mma. Ramotswe. "They lived in Mochudi. They were a big family. Many children."

"She is married to one of the sons of that family," said Mma. Potokwani. "He works for the Roads Department. He drives a steamroller. She told me that he ran over a dog with his steamroller last week, by mistake, of course. It was a very old dog, apparently, who did not hear the steamroller coming."

"That is very sad," said Mma. Ramotswe. "But the late dog would not have suffered. At least there is that."

Mma. Potokwani thought for a moment. "I suppose not," she said.

"This cake is delicious," said Mma. Ramotswe. "Perhaps Mma. Gotofede would teach me how to make it one day. Motholeli and Puso would like it."

Mma. Potokwani smiled at the mention of the children. "I hope that they are doing well," she said. "It is very kind of you and Mr. J.L.B. Matekoni to adopt them like that."

Mma. Ramotswe lifted her teacup and looked at Mma. Potokwani over the rim. There had never been any mention of adoption before this; the agreement had been to foster them, had it not? Not that it made much difference, but you had to watch Mma. Potokwani: she would do anything to benefit the orphans.

"We are happy to have them," said Mma. Ramotswe. "They can live with us until they are grown up. Motholeli wants to be a mechanic, by the way. Did you know that? She is very good with machines, and Mr. J.L.B. Matekoni is going to teach her."

Mma. Potokwani clapped her hands with delight. She was ambitious for the orphans, and nothing gave her greater pleasure than to hear that one of the children was doing well in life. "That is such good news," she said. "Why can't a girl become a mechanic? Even if she is in a wheelchair. I am very happy to hear that news. She'll be able to help Mr. J.L.B. Matekoni fix our pump."

"He is going to make a ramp for her wheelchair," said Mma. Ramotswe. "Then she will be able to get at the engines."

Mma. Potokwani nodded her approval of the plan. "And her brother?" she said. "Is he doing well, too?"

She knew from Mma. Ramotswe's hesitation that something was wrong.

"What's the matter? Is he not well?"

"It's not that," said Mma. Ramotswe. "He is eating well and he is growing. Already I have bought him new shoes. There is nothing wrong there. It's just that. . . ."

"Behaviour?" prompted Mma. Potokwani.

Mma. Ramotswe nodded. "I didn't want to bother you with it, but I thought that you might be able to advise me. You have seen every sort of child there is. You know all about children."

"They are all different," agreed Mma. Potokwani. "Brother and sister—it makes no difference. The recipe for each child is just for that child, even if it is the same mother and father. One child is fat, one child is thin. One child is clever, one is not that clever. So it goes on. Every child is different."

"He started off as a good little boy," said Mma. Ramotswe. "He was polite and he did nothing wrong. And then, suddenly, he started to do bad things. We have not smacked him or anything like that, but he has become very sullen and resentful. He glowers at me sometimes and I do not know what to do."

Mma. Potokwani listened attentively as Mma. Ramotswe went on to describe some of the incidents which had taken place, including the killing of the hoopoe with the catapult.

"He did not learn to kill birds here," said Mma. Potokwani firmly. "We do not allow the children to kill animals. They are taught that the animals are their brothers and sisters. That is what we do."

"And when Mr. J.L.B. Matekoni spoke to him about it, he said that he hated him."

"Hated?" exclaimed Mma. Potokwani. "Nobody should hate Mr. J.L.B. Matekoni, and certainly not a little boy who has been given a home by him, and by you."

"It is as if somebody has poured poison into his ear," said Mma. Ramotswe.

Mma. Potokwani reached forward and refilled Mma. Ramotswe's teacup, frowning as she did so. "That is probably more true than you think, Mma. Poison in the ear. It happens to all children."

"I do not understand," said Mma. Ramotswe. "When could this have happened?"

"He goes to school now, doesn't he? Children go to school and they discover that there are other children. Not all these children behave well. Some of them are bad children. They are the ones with the poison."

Mma. Ramotswe remembered what Motholeli had told her about the bullying. Puso was much younger, of course, but could be experiencing the same thing.

"I think that he doesn't know where he stands," said Mma. Potokwani. "He will know that he is different from the other boys at school—because he's an orphan—but he will have no idea how to make up for that. So he's blaming you because he's lost."

Mma. Ramotswe thought that this sounded reasonable, but

then what could they do? They had tried to be kind to him and give him more attention, but that seemed to have no effect.

I think," said Mma. Potokwani, "that it is time for Mr. J.L.B. Matekoni to start giving him some rules to live by. He needs to show him limits. Other boys will have fathers or uncles to do that. They need it." She paused, watching the effect of her words on Mma. Ramotswe. "He needs to be more of a father, I suspect. He needs to be stronger. His trouble is that he is such a gentle, kind man. We all know that. But that might not be what that little boy needs."

Mma. Ramotswe became very thoughtful. "Mr. J.L.B. Matekoni must be firmer?"

Mma. Potokwani smiled. "A bit. But what he needs to do is to take the boy out with him in his truck. Take him out to the lands, to see the cattle. Things like that."

"I shall tell him," said Mma. Ramotswe.

Mma. Potokwani put her teacup down and looked out of the window again. A group of children was playing under a shady jacaranda tree. "You can find out everything you want about children by watching them play," she said. "Look at those children over there. You'll see that the boys are playing together, pushing one another over, and the girls are watching. They will want to join in, but they won't know how to do it, and they're not very keen on that rough game. See? Can you see what's happening?"

Mma. Ramotswe looked out. She saw the boys—a group of five or six of them—engaged in their physical play. She saw one of the girls pointing at the boys and then stepping forward to say something to them. The boys ignored her.

"See," said Mma. Potokwani. "If you want to understand the world, just look out there. Those boys are just playing, but it's very serious to them. They're finding out who the leader is going to be.

That tall boy there, you see him, he's the leader. He'll be doing the same thing in ten, twenty years' time."

"And the girls?" asked Mma. Ramotswe. "Why are they just standing there?"

Mma. Potokwani laughed. "They think the game is silly, but they would like to join in. They are watching the boys. Then they will work out some way of spoiling the boys' fun. They will get better and better at that."

"I am sure that you are right," said Mma. Ramotswe.

"I think I am," Mma. Potokwani said. "We had somebody out from the university, you know. This person called herself a psychologist. She had studied in America, and she had read many books about how children grow up. I said: just look out of the window. She did not know what I meant, but I think that you do, Mma. Ramotswe."

"Yes," said Mma. Ramotswe. "I do."

You don't have to read a book to understand how the world works," Mma. Potokwani continued. "You just have to keep your eyes open."

"That's true," agreed Mma. Ramotswe. But she had her reservations about Mma. Potokwani's assertions. She had a great respect for books herself, and she wished that she had read more. One could never read enough. Never.

CHAPTER FOURTEEN

MR. BERNARD SELELIPENG

YOU WERE very brave back there," said Mma. Ramotswe to Mr. J.L.B. Matekoni as they travelled back from the orphan farm. "It is not easy to stand up to Mma. Potokwani, and you did it."

Mr. J.L.B. Matekoni smiled. "I didn't think I would have the courage. But when I looked at the old pump, and heard it make those strange sounds, I decided that I just would not do it again. After all those repairs. There is a time to let a machine go."

"I watched her face as you told her," said Mma. Ramotswe. "She was very surprised. It was as if one of the children had spoken back to her. She had not expected it."

In spite of her surprise, though, Mma. Potokwani had given in remarkably quickly. There had been a halfhearted attempt to persuade Mr. J.L.B. Matekoni to change his mind and to fix the pump—"just for one last time"—but when she realised that he was adamant, she had switched to the question of who could be persuaded to pay for a new one. There was a general-purpose fund, of course, which was more than capable of footing the bill, but this would be drawn upon only when there was no other way of meeting the cost. Somewhere there would be somebody who might be persuaded that it would be an honour to have a pump named after them; that was always a good way of getting funds. Some people liked to do good by stealth, discreetly and anonymously providing funds, but others liked to do their charitable works in the glare of as much publicity as Mma. Potokwani could arrange. This did not matter, of course: the important thing was to get the pump.

Mr. J.L.B. Matekoni had not left the orphan farm without making a positive contribution. Although he had brought bad tidings about the pump, he had nonetheless spent an hour attending to a timing problem in the engine of the old blue minivan used to transport the orphans. Again, this could not be kept going indefinitely, and he wondered when he would have to announce its end to Mma. Potokwani, but for the time being he could keep it on the road with judicious tinkering.

While he worked on the van, Mma. Ramotswe and Mma. Potokwani had occupied themselves by visiting some of the housemothers. Mma. Gotofede had been consulted about her recipe for fruitcake and had written it out for Mma. Ramotswe and given her one or two tips on how to ensure the right consistency and moisture level. Then they had seen the new laundry, and Mma. Potokwani had demonstrated the efficiency of the steam irons which they had recently acquired.

"The children must always look neat," she had explained. "A neat child is happier than a scruffy child. That is a well-known fact."

It had been a good visit, and in the truck on the way back, after they had discussed the pump, Mma. Ramotswe judged the time right to raise with Mr. J.L.B. Matekoni the issue of Puso's behaviour. It would be a difficult message to convey. She did not want Mr. J.L.B. Matekoni to think that she was criticising him, or that Mma. Potokwani had done so, but she had to encourage him to play a greater role in the boy's life.

"I talked to her about Puso," she ventured. "She was sorry to hear that he had been difficult."

"Was she surprised?" he asked.

Mma. Ramotswe shook her head. "Not at all. She said that boys are difficult to raise. She said that men need to spend time with boys, to help them. If they do not, then boys can be confused and difficult. Somebody must spend more time with Puso."

"Me?" he said. "She must mean me."

Mma. Ramotswe wondered whether he was angry; it was hard to tell with Mr. J.L.B. Matekoni. She had seen him angry on one or two occasions, but be had controlled himself so well that one might have missed it.

"I suppose so," she said. "She suggested that you could do more things with him. In that way he would think of you more as his father. It would be good for him."

"Oh," said Mr. J.L.B. Matekoni. "I see. She must think that I am not a good father, then."

Mma. Ramotswe did not like to lie. She was a stout defender of the truth, but there were occasions on which a slight embroidering of reality was necessary in order to save another from hurt.

"Not at all," she said. "Mma. Potokwani said that you were the best father that boy could ever wish for. That's what she said."

It was not, but it could have been said by Mma. Potokwani. If she did not think this, then why had she been so keen to send the children to him in the first place? No, this was not a lie; it was an *interpretation.*

It had the hoped-for effect. Mr. J.L.B. Matekoni beamed with pleasure and scratched his head. "That was a kind thing for her to say. But I shall try to do more with him, as she suggests. I shall take him for rides in the truck."

"A good idea," said Mma. Ramotswe quickly. "And maybe you can play some games with him. Football, perhaps."

"Yes," said Mr. J.L.B. Matekoni. "I shall do all these things, starting this very evening. I shall do them."

When they returned to Zebra Drive, while Mma. Ramotswe prepared the evening meal, Mr. J.L.B. Matekoni took Puso for a ride in his truck to look at the dam, taking him onto his lap and allowing him to steer the wheel as they bumped along a back track. On the way home, they stopped at a café for potato chips, which they ate in the cab of the truck. Then they returned, and Mma. Ramotswe noticed that both were smiling.

THE NEXT day at the shared premises of the No. 1 Ladies' Detective Agency and Tlokweng Road Speedy Motors, everybody's mood, if not elevated, was at least buoyant. Mr. J.L.B. Matekoni felt considerable satisfaction at having prompted the purchase of a new pump at the orphan farm, and was happy, too, with the progress he had made in communicating with Puso. Mma. Ramotswe shared his pleasure in this and was further cheered when the morning post brought three cheques from clients who had been stalling in their payments. The younger apprentice had about him an air of quiet serenity, as if he had seen a vision, thought Mma. Ramotswe, although she could not work out what could have made him look so pleased with himself. The older apprentice was strangely silent—although in no sense grumpy. Something had happened to him, too, thought Mma. Ramotswe, although again she could not imagine what it was, unless, in his case, it had been the discovery of some breathtakingly beautiful girl who had stunned him into silence and contemplation.

The younger apprentice would very much have liked to spread the good news of the miracle which they had witnessed at Tlokweng Road Speedy Motors the previous afternoon. He could not do this—the garage at least—because of the compromising circumstances in which the miracle had occurred. To announce that prayer had caused the malfunctioning hydraulics to work would entail admitting that they had wrongfully used the equipment in the first place. Mr. J.L.B. Matekoni would probably not be so interested in how the car came down as he would be in how it came to be up in the air, and this would lead to a reprimand, at the very least, or possibly to a docking of pay, which he was entitled to do under their apprenticeship contract in the event of serious wrongdoing. So the apprentice could not announce that something special had happened, nor claim the credit for having caused this event. He would have to wait until the following Sunday, when he would be able to reveal to the congregation at the church, to the brothers and sisters who would be interested in this sort of thing, that prayer had brought immediate and concrete results.

The older apprentice was naturally sceptical about such things, but he had been astonished by what appeared to be a clear connection between a prayed-for event and the event itself. If his younger colleague could do this, then did it mean that everything else that he did was equally valid? This had alarming implications, as it meant that he would have to pay some attention to his predictions of divine wrath should he, Charlie, not change his ways. That was a sobering thought.

Mma. Ramotswe also noticed that there was something different about Mma. Makutsi. It could have been that she had new shoes and a new dress, both of which could do a great deal for a person's mood, but she thought that there was something more to it than that. What struck her was a certain demureness that appeared to have crept into her manner, and for this there was usually only one explanation.

"You are happy today, Mma.," she said casually, as she entered the details of the cheques in her cash-received book.

Mma. Makutsi made an airy movement with her right hand. "It is a nice day. We have received those cheques."

Mma. Ramotswe smiled. "Yes," she said. "But we have received cheques before, and they have not had this effect on you. There is something more, isn't there?"

"You're the detective," said Mma. Makutsi playfully. "You tell me what it is."

"You have met a man," said Mma. Ramotswe plainly. "That is how people behave when they have met a man."

Mma. Makutsi seemed deflated. "Oh," she said.

"There," said Mma. Ramotswe. "I knew it. I am very pleased, Mma. I hope that he is a nice man."

"Oh he is," enthused Mma. Makutsi. "He is a very handsome man. With a moustache. He has a moustache and his hair is parted in the middle."

"That is interesting," said Mma. Ramotswe. "I like moustaches, too." She wondered whether Mr. J.L.B. Matekoni would be persuaded to grow a moustache, but decided that it was unlikely. She had heard him talking to the apprentices about the need for mechanics to be clean-shaven; it was something to do with grease, she imagined.

She waited for Mma. Makutsi to enlarge on her description, but she sat at her desk, busying herself with a sheaf of garage bills. So she returned to her cash book.

"He has a very nice smile, too," Mma. Makutsi suddenly added. "That is one of the nice things about him."

"Oh yes?" said Mma. Ramotswe. "And have you been out dancing with him? Men with moustaches can be good dancers."

Mma. Makutsi lowered her voice. "We haven't actually been out together yet," she said. "But that will happen soon. Maybe tonight."

MR. BERNARD Selelipeng was the first student to arrive that evening, knocking at the door of the hall a good twenty minutes before the class was due to start. Mma. Makutsi had already been there for half an hour, setting out the papers for the evening's exercises and touching up the chalked-in finger diagram on the blackboard. A group of Boy Scouts had met in the hall that afternoon, and one of the Scouts had traced finger marks over Mma. Makutsi's drawing of the typewriter keyboard, necessitating some repairs to the third finger on the right hand and the little finger on the left.

"It's only me, Mma.," he said on entering the room. "Bernard Selelipeng."

She looked up and smiled at him. She noticed the gleaming parting in his hair and the neat buttoned-down collar. She saw, too, his highly polished shoes; another good sign, in her view, and one which suggested that he would appreciate her own new green shoes.

She smiled at him as he made his way over to his desk, to which she had earlier returned his essay. As he picked up the piece of paper and began to read her pencilled-in comment, she purported to concentrate on the pile of papers on her table, but she was watching for his reaction.

He looked up, and she knew immediately that she had done the right thing. Folding up his essay, he crossed the room to stand before her.

"I hope that you did not think I was being rude, Mma.," he said. "I wanted to write the truth, and that was the truth."

"Of course I did not think you rude," she said. "I was happy to read what you had written."

"And your reply is just what I was hoping for," he said. "I would like to ask you to come for a drink with me after the class tonight. Will you be free?"

Of course she would, and for the rest of the class, although she was outwardly occupied with the teaching of typing, she could not think of anything other than Mr. Bernard Selelipeng, and it was difficult to address questions to the class as a whole rather than to the smiling, elegant man seated in the middle of the second row. There were so many questions that had to be answered. What was his job, for example? Where was he from? How old was he? She guessed that he was in his mid- to late thirties, but it was always difficult to tell with men.

At the end, when the class had been dismissed and everybody except for Bernard Selelipeng and Mma. Makutsi had dispersed, he helped her to tidy up and to lock the hall. Then he showed her to his car, the possession of which was another good sign, and they drove off in the direction of a bar which he said he knew at the edge of the town, on the Francistown Road. It was an intensely pleasurable feeling for her, sitting in the passenger seat of his car, like any other of those fortunate women who were driven about by their husbands and lovers with such an air of security and possession. It seemed to her to feel completely right, that she should be transported in this way, a handsome, moustachioed man at the wheel. How quickly, too, one might become accustomed to this; no long walk to work across dusty paths, trodden by so many other feet, nor any frustrating wait for the crowded and stuffy minibuses which would ferry one about in bone-shaking discomfort for a pula or two.

Bernard Selelipeng glanced at her and flashed his smile in her direction. The smile, she thought, was his most attractive feature. It was a warm, inviting smile, of the sort that one could imagine living with. A husband who scowled all the time would be worse than no husband at all, but a man who smiled like that would turn his wife weak at the knees every day.

They arrived at the bar. Mma. Makutsi had seen it before,

from the road, but had never been in. It was an expensive place, she had heard, where you could have a meal, too, if you wished. There was music playing in the background as they went in, and a waiter quickly appeared to take their order. Bernard Selelipeng ordered a beer, and Mma. Makutsi, who never drank alcohol, ordered a soft drink with ice.

Bernard Selelipeng knocked his glass gently against hers and smiled again. They had not made much conversation in the car, and now he asked her politely where she lived and what she did for a living during the day. Mma. Makutsi was not sure whether she should tell him about the No. 1 Ladies' Detective Agency, as she was not certain whether he would be inhibited by her being a detective, even if only an assistant detective, and so she confined herself to mentioning her role as the assistant manager of Tlokweng Road Speedy Motors.

"And what about you, Rra.?" she asked. "What do you do yourself?"

"I work in the diamond office," he said. "I am a personnel manager there."

This impressed Mma. Makutsi. Jobs with the diamond company were well paid and secure, and it was a good thing, she thought, to be a personnel manager, which had a modern ring to it. But even as she thought this, she wondered why a personnel manager, handsome, of an interesting age, and in possession of his own car, should be unattached. He must be one of the most eligible men in Gaborone, and yet he was paying attention to her, Mma. Makutsi, who was not necessarily the most glamorous of ladies. He could go to the Botswana Secretarial College, park outside the drive, and pick up any number of fashionable girls much younger than herself. And yet he did not. She glanced at his left hand as he lifted his glass of beer to his mouth. There was no ring.

"I live by myself," said Bernard Selelipeng. "I have a flat in one of those blocks at the edge of the village. That's not far from your garage. That's where I live."

"They are very nice flats," said Mma. Makutsi.

"I would like to show you my place someday," said Bernard Selelipeng. "I think you would like it."

"But why do you live by yourself?" asked Mma. Makutsi. "Most people would get lonely living by themselves."

"I am divorced," said Bernard Selelipeng. "My wife went away with another man and took our children with her. That is why I am by myself."

Mma. Makutsi was astonished that any woman could leave a man like this, but of course she might well have been the flashy type, and they were notorious. She imagined that such a wife could have her head turned by a richer, more successful man— although Bernard Selelipeng was clearly successful.

They made easy conversation for several hours. He was witty and entertaining, and she laughed at his descriptions of some of his colleagues in the diamond office. She told him about the apprentices, and he laughed at them. Then, shortly before ten o'clock, he looked at his watch and announced that he would be happy to run her home, as he had to be at an early meeting the following morning and did not wish to be too late. So they went back to the car and drove back through the night. Outside the house in which she rented her room, he stopped the car but did not turn off the engine. Again this was a good sign.

"Good night," he said, touching her gently on the shoulder. "I will see you at the class tomorrow."

She smiled at him encouragingly. "You have been very kind," she said. "Thank you for this evening."

"I cannot wait for us to go out again," he said. "There is a film I would like to see at the cinema. Perhaps we can go to that."

"I would like that very much," said Mma. Makutsi.

She watched him drive down the road, the rear red lights of his car disappearing in the darkness. She sighed; he was so kind, so gentlemanly, rather like a glamorous version of Mr. J.L.B. Matekoni. What a coincidence it was that she and Mma. Ramotswe should both have found such good men, when there were so many charlatans and deceivers about.

CHAPTER FIFTEEN

A DISGRUNTLED CLIENT

W ITH SUCH a profusion of positive developments, they had given little thought to the rival agency, and perhaps they would have forgotten about it completely had it not been for two developments which reminded them of Mr. Buthelezi. The first of these was an interview published in the *Botswana Gazette,* an interview which took up the entire features page and was headed by a picture of Mr. Buthelezi sitting at his desk, a cigarette in one hand and the telephone hand-piece in the other. The article was spotted by Mma. Ramotswe, who read it out to Mma. Makutsi while the latter sipped thoughtfully, but with increasing astonishment, at a mug of bush tea.

"From New York to Gaborone, via Johannesburg," ran the caption at the top of the page. "A detective from different worlds: we spoke to the charming Mr. Buthelezi in his well-appointed office, and asked him what it was like to be a private detective in Gaborone.

"'It is quite hard being the first proper detective,' he said. 'There are, as people know, one or two ladies who have been dabbling in this for a little while, but they have no background in detection. I am not saying that there is not a job for them to do.

There will always be jobs relating to children and the like. I am sure that they will do those very well. But for the real work, you need a proper detective.

"'I was trained with the CID in Johannesburg. That was a very tough training, with all those gangsters and all those murders, but I soon learned to be tough. You have to be tough in this business. That's why men are best at it. They're tougher than women.

"'I had many cases in the CID. Well-known murders. Jewel thefts. Ow! Millions of rands gone, just like that! Kidnappings, too. All of that was my daily bread, and I soon found that I understood the criminal mind very well. That's experience for you.

"'I have been very busy since I opened up. There are obviously many problems here in this city, and so if any readers have something that needs looking into, I am their man. I repeat, I am their man.

"'You ask what are the best qualities for a private detective? I would say that an understanding of how human psychology works is one of the best. Then a good eye for detail. We have to notice things—often very little things—in order to find out the truth for our clients. So a private detective is like a camera, always taking photographs in his mind and always trying to understand what is going on. That is the secret.

"'You ask how you become a private detective? The answer is that you have to be trained, preferably in the CID. You cannot just set up your sign and say that you are a private detective. Some people have tried that, even here in Gaborone, but that will never work. You have to have been trained.

"'It's also helpful if you've been to London or New York, or to some of those places. If you've done that, then you know the world, and nobody will be able to pull the wool over your eyes. I have I been in New York, and I know all about the private detection side of things there. I know many of the men working in this area. They are very clever men, these New York detectives, and we were close friends.

"'But at the end of the day, I always say, East West, Home's Best! That is why I am back here in Gaborone, which was my mother's place and which was where I went to school. I am a Motswana detective with a strange name. I know a lot, and what I don't know, I'll soon find out. Give me a call. Anytime!'"

Mma. Ramotswe finished reading and then tossed the newspaper down with disgust. She was used to bragging men, and was tolerant of them, but these words from Mr. Buthelezi went too far. All those references to the superiority of men over women in detection were unambiguously aimed at her and her agency, and while it was obvious that an attack of this sort could only be the result of insecurity on his part, it could hardly be left unanswered. And yet an answer was probably what he wanted, as it would merely draw further attention to his business. Moreover—and this was worrying—what he said would probably strike a chord with many of the newspaper's readers. She suspected that there were plenty of people who did believe that the work which she did was better done by a man. They believed this of driving and flying aeroplanes, in spite of the fact that she had read—and others surely had read, too—of the evidence that women are simply safer drivers and pilots than men. The reason for this, apparently, is that they are more cautious and less given to flamboyant risk-taking. That is why women, on the whole, drive more slowly than men. Yet many men refused to acknowledge this fact and made belittling remarks about women's driving.

"I'm going to do a little bit of research," she said to Mma. Makutsi. "Could you go and fetch Charlie, Mma. I want him to read this."

Mma. Makutsi looked puzzled. "Why?" she asked. "You know that he's only interested in girls. He won't be interested in this."

"An experiment," said Mma. Ramotswe. "You wait and see."

Mma. Makutsi left the office and came back a few minutes later with the older apprentice, who was wiping his hands on the cotton lint that Mr. J.L.B. Matekoni provided in his battle against grease.

"Yes, Mma.," said the apprentice. "Mma. Makutsi says you need my advice. I am always happy to give advice. Ha!"

Mma. Ramotswe ignored the comment.

"You read this, please," she said. "I would like to get your opinion on it."

She handed him the newspaper, pointing to the article, and the apprentice sat down on the chair in front of her desk. As he read, his lips moved, and Mma. Ramotswe watched the look of concentration on his face. *He never reads a newspaper,* she thought. *There really is nothing in that head but thoughts of girls and cars.*

When he had finished, the apprentice looked up at Mma. Ramotswe.

"I have read it now, Mma.," he said, handing the paper back to her. She saw the greasy fingerprints on the edges and delicately avoided touching them.

"What do you think of it, Charlie?" she asked.

He shrugged. "I am sorry, Mma.," he said. "I am sorry for you."

"Sorry?"

"Yes," he expanded. "I am sorry that this is going to make it difficult for your business. Everybody will go to that man now."

"So you were impressed?"

He smiled. "Of course. That is a very clever man there. New York. Did you see that. And Johannesburg. All those places. He knows what is happening, and he will deal with many things. I am sorry, because I do not want the business to go to him."

"You are very loyal," said Mma. Ramotswe. And then, as the apprentice rose to his feet and left the room, she thought: *Exactly!*

"Well, Mma.," said Mma. Ramotswe. "That shows us something, doesn't it?"

Mma. Makutsi made a dismissive gesture. "That boy is stupid. We all know that. Don't believe anything he says."

"He's not that stupid," said Mma. Ramotswe. "To get the apprenticeship, he had to pass exams. He is probably a fairly average young man. So, you see, many, many people will be impressed by this Mr. Buthelezi. We cannot change that fact."

MANY PEOPLE, perhaps, but not all. That afternoon, when Mma. Makutsi had been dispatched to the births, deaths, and marriages registry to pursue some routine enquiries on behalf of a client, Mma. Ramotswe was visited, unannounced, by a woman whose view of the Satisfaction Guaranteed Agency and its boastful proprietor was quite the opposite of the view held by the apprentice. She arrived in a smart new car, which she parked directly outside the agency door, and waited politely for Mma. Ramotswe to acknowledge her presence before she entered the office. This always pleased Mma. Ramotswe; she could not abide the modern habit of entering a room before being asked to do so, or, even worse, the assumption that some people made that they could come into your office uninvited and actually sit on your desk while they spoke. If that happened to her, she would refrain from speaking at all but would look pointedly at the bottom planted upon her desk until her disapproval registered and it was removed.

Her visitor was a woman somewhere in her late thirties, about Mma. Ramotswe's own age, even slightly younger. She was dressed well but not flashily, and her clothing, together with the new car outside, told Mma. Ramotswe all that she needed to know about her economic circumstances. This woman, she imagined, was a well-paid senior civil servant, or even a business-woman.

"I have no appointment, Mma.," said the woman, "but I hoped that you would be able to see me anyway."

Mma. Ramotswe smiled. "I am always happy to see people, Mma. An appointment is not necessary. I am happy to talk at any time," adding: "within reason."

The woman accepted Mma. Ramotswe's invitation to sit down. She had not given her name, although she had used the correct greeting; doubtless, the name would emerge later.

"I must be truthful, Mma.," she said. "I have no confidence in private detectives. I must tell you that."

Mma. Ramotswe raised an eyebrow. If she had no confidence in private detectives, then why would she come to the No. 1 Ladies' Detective Agency, the name of which was sufficiently self-explanatory, she would have thought.

"I am sorry to hear that, Mma.," she said. "Maybe you would tell me why."

The woman now looked slightly apologetic. "Not that I mean to be rude, Mma. It's just that I have had a very unpleasant experience with a detective agency. That is why I feel as I do."

Mma. Ramotswe nodded. "The Satisfaction Guranteed Agency? Mr. Buthele—"

She did not have the time to finish. "Yes," said the woman. "That man! How he thinks that he can call himself a private detective, I do not know."

Mma. Ramotswe was intrigued. She wished that Mma. Makutsi had been present, as it would have been good to share with her whatever was about to be disclosed. And it was going to be choice, she thought. But before she allowed her visitor to explain, the idea occurred to her that she should make an offer, on behalf of the entire profession. Yes, it was just the right thing to do in the circumstances.

"Let me say one thing, Mma.," she said, raising her hand. "If you have suffered at the hands of a fellow member of my profession—and I must say that I am not surprised to hear this—then the No. 1 Ladies' Detective Agency will undertake to complete the enquiry which Mr. Buthe . . . which that man has obviously not done properly. That is my offer."

The woman was clearly impressed. "You are very good, Mma. I did not come expecting that, but I am happy to accept your offer. I can tell that things are different in this place."

"They are," said Mma. Ramotswe quietly. "We do not make claims that we cannot live up to. We are not like that."

"Good," said the woman. "Now, let me tell you what happened."

SHE HAD gone to see Mr. Buthelezi after seeing his advertisement in the newspaper. He had been very polite to her, although she had found his manner rather overwhelming.

"But I thought that this might be something to do with the name," she said, glancing at Mma. Ramotswe, who nodded, almost imperceptibly. One had to be careful about what one said, but people understood, and they knew what Zulu people could be like. Perhaps the word was . . . well, *pushy* or, if one were a bit more charitable, *self-confident*. Not that one liked to make such remarks openly, of course. Mr. Buthelezi said that he was a Motswana and not a Zulu, but you could not ignore paternal ancestry that easily, especially if you were a man. It stood to reason, Mma. Ramotswe thought, that boys took more after their father than their mother; could people seriously doubt that? Some did, apparently, but they were obviously wrong.

The woman went on to explain why she had been to see Mr. Buthelezi in the first place.

"I live in Mochudi," she said, "although I am originally from Francistown. I am a physiotherapist at the hospital there. I work with people who have broken limbs or who have been very ill and need help in getting back on their feet. That is one of the things we do, but there are others. It is a very good job."

"And very important," said Mma. Ramotswe. "You must be proud to be a physiotherapist, Mma."

The woman nodded. "I am. Anyway, I live up there because that is where the job is. I also have four children, and they are happy at the school there. The only problem is that my husband has a job in town here and he did not like driving in from Mochudi every morning and back again. We put our savings into a small flat. I get my house in Mochudi with the job, so this seemed like a good thing to do."

It was at this point that Mma. Ramotswe realised what was coming. Ever since she had opened the No. 1 Ladies' Detective Agency, she had received a regular stream of requests to deal with errant husbands, or husbands suspected of being errant. These wifely fears were usually well founded, and Mma. Ramotswe had been obliged to be the bearer of news of infidelity rather more often than she might have wished. But that was part of the job, and she did it with dignity and compassion. She was sure that this was what her new client was about to disclose; husbands working away from home rarely behaved themselves, although some, a small number, did.

Mma. Ramotswe was right. The woman now described her fears about her husband and how she was sure that he was seeing somebody else.

"I usually telephone him in the evenings," she said. "We talk about things that have happened during the day, and the children also speak to him. It is expensive, but it is important for the children to talk to their daddy. But now he is never in when I call. He says that this is because he is now enjoying walking, and he goes for a lot of walks, but that is nonsense. I can tell that this is a lie."

"It sounds like it," said Mma. Ramotswe. "Some men cannot lie very well."

The woman had consulted Mr. Buthelezi about her concerns, and he had promised to look into the matter, telling her to get back in touch with him after a day or so. He said that he would follow the husband and let her know what he was up to.

"And did he?" asked Mma. Ramotswe. She was eager to hear how her rival operated.

"He says that he did," said the woman. "But I do not believe him. He says that he followed him and that he is going to church. That is just ridiculous. My husband does not go to church. I have tried and tried to make him go, but he is lazy about it. And when he came home last weekend, I said to him on Sunday: 'Let's go to church.' And he said that he did not want to go. Now, if he had become a great churchgoer, then surely he would want to go on a Sunday. But he did not. That proves it, in my mind."

Mma. Ramotswe had to agree.

"But there is something more," said the woman. "I had paid a very large fee in advance, and when I said that I thought I should get some of it back, Mr. Buthe . . . that man just refused. He said that the money was his now. So I came to you."

Mma. Ramotswe smiled. "I will do my best. I will see whether this churchgoing is true, and, if it isn't—and I agree with you that it does not sound likely—then I shall find out what he really is doing, and I shall tell you all about it."

They discussed one or two further details, including the name and address of the husband, and the address of the place where he worked.

"I have brought you a photograph, too," the woman said. "It will help you to recognize him."

She passed over a black-and-white photograph of a man looking into the camera. Mma. Ramotswe glanced at it and saw a neatly attired man with an engaging smile, a carefully tended centre parting, and a moustache. She had never seen him before, but he would be easily picked out from a crowd.

"This will be very useful, Mma.," she said. "When clients do not provide photographs, our work can be more difficult."

Mma. Selelipeng rose to her feet.

"I am very cross with him," she said. "But I know that once I find this lady who is trying to steal my husband, I shall be able to deal with her. I shall teach her a lesson."

Mma. Ramotswe frowned.

"You must not do anything illegal," she said. "I will not help you if that is what you are planning."

Mma. Selelipeng raised her hands in horror. "No, nothing like that, Mma. I would just be planning to speak to her. To warn her. That is all. Don't you think that any woman has a right to do that?"

Mma. Ramotswe nodded. She had no time for husband stealers, and no time for deceiving men. People had the right to protect what was theirs, but she was a kind woman and understood human weakness. This Mr. Bernard Seletipeng probably needed no more than a gentle reminder of his duties as a husband and a father. Looking at the photograph again, she suspected that this would suffice. It was not a strong face, she thought; it was not the face of a man who would leave his wife for good. He would go back like a naughty boy who has been caught stealing melons. She was sure of it.

CHAPTER SIXTEEN

MMA. RAMOTSWE GETS A FLAT TYRE;
MMA. MAKUTSI GOES TO THE CINEMA
WITH MR. BERNARD SELELIPENG

MMA. RAMOTSWE was driving back to Zebra Drive that evening, taking her normal route from the Tlokweng Road and turning off into Odi Drive, when the tiny white van began to pull over to the left. She wondered for a moment whether the steering was faulty, and she shifted her weight in the seat towards the right, but this made no difference. Now there was a strange sound coming from the back of the van, a grinding sound, as of metal on stone, and she realised that she had a flat tyre. This was both an annoyance and a relief at the same time, the relief coming from the fact that it was an easily tackled problem. If one had a spare wheel, that is, and she did not. She had asked one of the apprentices to take it out for inflating, and she had seen it propped up against the wall of the garage and had been on the point of putting it back when Mma. Makutsi had called her inside to take a telephone call. So the spare wheel remained in Tlokweng Road Speedy Motors, and she was here, on the side of the road, where it was needed.

She felt a momentary irritation with herself. There was really no excuse for driving without a spare wheel; tyres were always going flat with all those sharp stones on the road and dropped nails and the like. If it had happened to somebody else, she would have had no hesitation in saying: Well, it's not very clever, is it, to drive a car without a spare wheel; and here it had happened to her, and she richly deserved such self-reproach.

She drew over to the left, to keep the car away from the traffic, not that there was much of that along this quiet residential road. She looked about her. She was not far from Zebra Drive— about half an hour's walk, at the most—and she could easily walk home and wait for Mr. J.L.B. Matekoni to come round for dinner. Then they could rescue the tiny white van together. Or, and this made more sense in terms of avoiding extra journeys, she could telephone him at Tlokweng Road Speedy Motors, where he was working late, and ask him to bring the spare wheel with him on his way to Zebra Drive.

She looked about her. There was a public telephone in the shopping centre at the end of the road, or, and this was the obvious answer, there was Dr. Moffat's house, close to which the tiny white van was now parked. Dr. Moffat, who had helped Mr. J.L.B. Matekoni recover from his depressive illness, lived with his wife in a rambling old house, surrounded by a generous-sized garden, the gate of which Mma. Ramotswe now opened tentatively, bearing in mind how careful one had to be about dogs in yards like that. But there was no dog barking defiance, only the surprised voice of Mrs. Moffat, who emerged from behind a shrub which she had been tending.

"Mma. Ramotswe! You are always creeping up on people!"

Mma. Ramotswe smiled. "I am not here on business," she said. "I am here because my van out there has a flat tyre and I need to phone Mr. J.L.B. Matekoni for help. Would you mind, Mma.?"

Mrs. Moffat slipped her garden secateurs into her pocket. "We can telephone straightaway," she said. "And then we can have a cup of tea while we are waiting for Mr. J.L.B. Matekoni."

They went into the house, where Mma. Ramotswe telephoned Mr. J.L.B. Matekoni, told him of her misfortune, and explained where she was. Then, invited by the doctor's wife to join her on the verandah, they sat around a small table and talked.

There was much to talk about. Mrs. Moffat had lived in Mochudi when her husband had run the small hospital there, and she had known Obed Ramotswe and many of the families who were friendly with the Ramotswes. Mma. Ramotswe liked nothing more than to talk about those days, long past now, but so important to her sense of who she was.

"Do you remember my father's hat?" she asked, stirring sugar into her tea. "He wore the same hat for many years. It was very old."

"I remember it," said Mrs. Moffat. "The doctor used to describe it as a very wise hat."

Mma. Ramotswe laughed. "I suppose a hat sees many things," she said. "It must learn something." She paused. The memory was coming back to her of the day that her father lost his hat. He had taken it off for some reason and had forgotten where he had left it. For the best part of a day they had gone round Mochudi, trying to remember where he might have left it, asking people whether they had seen it. And at last it had been found on a wall near the kgotla, placed there by somebody who must have picked it up from the road. Would somebody in Gaborone put a hat in a safe place if it were found in the road? She thought not. We do not care about other people's hats in the same way these days, do we? We do not.

"I miss Mochudi," said Mrs. Moffat. "I miss those mornings when we listened to the cattle bells. I miss hearing the singing of the children from the school when the wind was in the right direction."

"It is a good place," said Mma. Ramotswe. "I miss listening to people talking about very small things."

"Like hats," ventured Mrs. Moffat.

"Yes, like hats. And special cattle. And which babies have arrived and what they are called. All those things."

Mrs. Moffat refilled the teacups, and for a few minutes they sat in easy silence, each with her own thoughts. Mma. Ramotswe thought of her father, and of Mochudi, and her childhood, and of how happy it had been even without a mother. And Mrs. Moffat thought of her parents, and of her father, an artist who had become blind, and of how hard it must have been to move into a world of darkness.

"I have some photographs which may interest you," Mrs. Moffat said after a while. "There are some photographs of Mochudi in those days. You will know the people in them."

She went off into the living room and returned with a large cardboard box.

"I have been meaning to put these into albums," she said, "but I have never got round to it. I shall do it one day, maybe."

"I am the same," said Mma. Ramotswe. "I will do these things one day."

The photographs were taken out and examined, one by one. There were many people Mma. Ramotswe remembered; here was Mrs. de Kok, the wife of the missionary, standing in front of a rosebush; here was the schoolteacher from the primary school giving a prize to a small child; here was the doctor himself playing tennis. And there, in a group of men in front of the kgotla, was Obed Ramotswe himself, wearing his hat, and the sight made her catch her breath.

"There," said Mrs. Moffat. "That's your father, isn't it?"

Mma. Ramotswe nodded.

"You take that," said Mrs. Moffat, handing her the photograph.

She accepted the gift gratefully and they looked at more photographs.

"Who is this?" asked Mma. Ramotswe, pointing to a photograph of an elderly woman sitting at a table in a shady part of a garden, playing cards with the Moffat children.

"That is the doctor's mother," said Mrs. Moffat.

"And this person standing behind them? This man who is looking at the camera?"

"That is somebody who comes to stay with us from time to time," said Mrs. Moffat. "He writes books."

Mma. Ramotswe examined the photograph more closely. "It seems that he is looking at me," she said. "He is smiling at me."

"Yes," said Mrs. Moffat. "Maybe he is."

Mma. Ramotswe looked again at the photograph of her father which Mrs. Moffat had given to her. Yes, that was his smile; hesitant at first, and then broader and broader; and his hat, of course . . . She wondered what the occasion had been, why these people were standing outside the gate of the kgotla, the meeting place; the doctor would know, perhaps, as he must have taken the photograph. Perhaps it was something to do with the hospital; people raised money for it and had meetings about it. That might have been it.

Everybody in the photograph was smartly dressed, even under the sun, and everybody was looking at the camera with *courtesy,* with an attitude of moral attention. That was the old Botswana way—to deal with others in this way—and that was passing, was it not, just as the world and the people captured in this photograph were passing. She touched the photograph with her finger, briefly, as if to communicate with, to touch, those in it, and as she did so, she felt her eyes fill with tears.

"Please excuse me, Mma.," she said to Mrs. Moffat. "I am thinking of how this old Botswana is going away."

"I understand," said Mrs. Moffat, reaching out for her friend's arm. "But we remember it, don't we?" And she thought, yes, this woman, this daughter of Obed Ramotswe, whom everybody agreed was a good man, would remember things about the old Botswana, about that country that had been—and still was— a beacon of light in Africa, a country of integrity and generosity in both the simple and the big things.

THAT EVENING the typing class went particularly well. Mma. Makutsi had planned a test for her students, to determine their speed, and had been pleasantly surprised by the results. One or two of the men were not very good—indeed, one of them was talking about giving up but had been persuaded by the other members of the class to persist. Most, however, had worked hard and were beginning to feel the benefits of practice and the expert tuition provided by Mma. Makutsi. Mr. Bernard Selelipeng was doing particularly well and, entirely on the basis of merit, had attained the highest words-per-minute score in the class.

"Very good, Mr. Selelipeng," said Mma. Makutsi as she looked at his score. She was determined to keep their professional relationship formal, although as she spoke to him, she felt a warm flush of feeling for this man who treated her with such respect and admiration. And he, in turn, treated her as his teacher, not as his girlfriend; there was no familiarity, no assumption that he would be given special treatment.

After the class ended and she had locked the hall, Mma. Makutsi went outside and found him, as they had agreed, sitting in his car, waiting for her. He suggested that they go to the cinema that evening, and afterwards to a café for something to eat. This idea appealed to Mma. Makutsi, who relished the thought that rather than going to the cinema by herself, as was often her lot, she would this time be sitting with a man, like most of the other women.

The film was full of silly, rich people living in conditions of unimaginable luxury, but Mma. Makutsi was barely interested in it and scarcely followed what was happening on screen. Her thoughts were with Mr. Bernard Selelipeng, who, halfway through the performance, slipped his hand into hers and whispered something heady into her ear. She felt excited and happy. Romance had arrived in her life at last, after all these years and all that waiting; a man had come to her and given her life a new meaning. That impression—or delusion—so common to lovers, of personal transformation, was strong upon her, and she closed her eyes at the sheer pleasure and happiness of it all. She would make him happy, this man who was so kind to her.

They went to a café after the cinema and ordered a meal. Then, sitting at a table near the door, they talked about one another, as lovers do, their hands joined under the table. That is where they were when Mma. Ramotswe came in, with Mr. J.L.B. Matekoni. Mma. Makutsi introduced her friend to Mma. Ramotswe, who smiled and greeted him politely.

Mma. Ramotswe and Mr. J.L.B. Matekoni did not stay long in the café.

"You are upset about something," said Mr. J.L.B. Matekoni to Mma. Ramotswe as they made their way back to the van.

"I am very sad," said Mma. Ramotswe. "I have found something out. But I am too upset to talk about it. Please drive me back to my house, Mr. J.L.B. Matekoni. I am very sad."

CHAPTER SEVENTEEN

FINDING TEBOGO

Y ES, THOUGHT Mma. Ramotswe, the world can be very discouraging. But we cannot sit and think about all the things that have gone wrong, or could go wrong. There was no point in doing that because it only made things worse. There was much for which we could be grateful, whatever the sorrows of this world. Besides, dwelling on the trials and tribulations of life was time-consuming, and ordinary duties still have to be performed; livings have to be earned, and in the case of Mma. Ramotswe, this meant that she had to do something about Mr. Molefelo and his conscience. It was over a week since she had found Mma. Tsolamosese, which had been the easy part; now she had to find Tebogo, the girl who had been so badly treated by Mr. Molefelo.

The information she had was slender, but if Tebogo had become a nurse, then she would have been registered, and might be registered still. That would be a starting point, and then, if Mma. Ramotswe found nothing there, she still had various other lines of enquiry. Tebogo had come from Molepolole, Mma. Ramotswe had been told. She could go there and find somebody who knew the family.

It did not take her long to exhaust the nursing route. Once

she had found the civil servant in charge of nurse training, it had been easy to ascertain whether anybody of that name had been registered as a nurse in Botswana. There had not, which meant that Tebogo had either not trained or, having been trained, had not completed her registration. Mma. Ramotswe was thoughtful; it might be that the consequences of Tebogo's involvement with Mr. Molefelo had had much greater repercussions for her life than she had imagined. People's lives are delicate; you cannot interfere with them without running the risk of changing them profoundly. A chance remark, a careless involvement, may make the difference between a life of happiness and one of sorrow.

A trip out to Molepolole would not be unwelcome and would give Mma. Ramotswe the chance to speak to several old friends whom she knew out there. One, in particular, a retired bankteller, knew everybody in the town and would be able to tell her about Tebogo's family. Perhaps Tebogo herself would be living there now, and Mma. Ramotswe would be able to visit her. That would require tact, particularly if she married. She might not have told her husband about the baby, and men can be possessive and unreasonable about these things. They, of course, did not have to bear the children; they did not have to carry the babies around on their backs for the first few years; they did not have to attend to the daily, hourly, minute-by-minute needs of the baby, and yet they could have very strong views on the subject of babies.

She chose a fine morning for the trip out to Motepolole, a morning when the air was crisp and clean and the sun not too hot. As she drove, she thought of the events of the last few days, and in particular of the disturbing discovery she had made of Mma. Makutsi's involvement with Mr. Bernard Selelipeng. She had been shocked by what she had found out, and the following morning her dismay had been compounded when Mma. Makutsi had talked at some length about Mr. Selelipeng and about how well suited they were.

"I would have told you about this earlier," she said to her employer. "But I wanted to be sure first that this was going to last. I did not want to come to you and say that I had found the right man for me, and then to have to tell you, one week later, that it was all off. I did not want that."

As Mma. Makutsi spoke, Mma. Ramotswe's sense of foreboding grew. There was much to be said in favour of honesty; she could tell Mma. Makutsi right now what the truth of the matter was, and indeed not to do so would be to shelter her from information which she had the right to know. Would she not feel more betrayed, wondered Mma. Ramotswe, if she were to find out that she, Mma. Ramotswe, had known all along and not warned her that Mr. Selelipeng was married? If one could not get this information from a friend and colleague, then from whom might one expect it? And yet, to tell her now would be so brutal, and it would also preclude the possibility of doing something in the background to ease the pain of discovery—whatever that something might be.

She would just have to think about it further, although she knew that at the end of the day there was inevitably going to be disappointment for Mma. Makutsi, who could not be protected forever from the truth about Mr. Bernard Selelipeng. But then, she thought, did she know? She had assumed all along that he would have misled her into thinking that he was single, or divorced, but it might be that Mma. Makutsi knew full well that there was a wife and family in the background. Was this likely? If a person was desperate enough, she might well be prepared to take any man who came along, even one who was married. Now that she came to think of it, she knew of many cases where women had been quite prepared to consort with married men in the full knowledge of their matrimonial status, hoping, perhaps, to prise the man away from his wife or even calculating that this would never happen but at least they would have some fun along the way. Men would do the same thing, too, although they seemed less willing to share a woman with another man. But Mma. Ramotswe certainly knew of cases where men had conducted affairs with married women, fully aware of the fact that the woman would never leave her husband.

Would Mma. Makutsi do this, she wondered. She remembered the awkward conversation she had had with her not all that long ago, when Mma. Makutsi had remarked despairingly on the fact that it was no use trying to meet men in bars because they were all married. This suggested that she considered such men to be out of bounds. And yet, faced with such a man, particularly with a charming one with a centre parting and a winning smile; might she not, in such circumstances, decide that even if he was married, this was nonetheless her chance? Time was ticking by for Mma. Makutsi; soon younger men would no longer consider her, and then she would be left with only the possibility of an old man. Perhaps she did feel desperate; perhaps she was fully aware of the situation in which Mr. Bernard Selelipeng found himself. But no. No, thought Mma. Ramotswe, she was not. She would not have spoken to me with that enthusiasm had she known this was a relationship that could not go any further. She would have been guarded, or resigned, or even sad; she would not have been enthusiastic.

Mma. Ramotswe was pleased that she had to put such troubling thoughts to one side, as she had now arrived in Molepolole and had driven the tiny white van over the rutted track that led to the house of her old friend Mma. Ntombi Boko, formerly deputy chief teller of the Standard Bank in Gaborone, a position from which she had retired at the age of fifty-four to take up residence in Molepolole and to run there the local branch of the Botswana Rural Women's Association.

She found Mma. Boko at the side of her house, under a canvas awning which she had erected to create an informal shady porch. A small brick oven had been built there, and on the top of this was a large blackened saucepan.

Mma. Boko's greeting was warm. "Precious Ramotswe! Yes, it is you! I can see you, Mma.!"

"It is me," said Mma. Ramotswe. "I have come to see you."

"I am very glad," said Mma. Boko. "I was sitting here stirring this jam and thinking: Where is everybody today? Why has nobody come to talk to me?"

"And then I arrived," said Mma. Ramotswe. "Just in time." She knew that her friend was gregarious, and that a day without a chance to have a good gossip was a trial for her. Not that the gossip was at all malicious; Mma. Boko spoke ill of nobody but was nevertheless extremely interested in what others were doing. Impressed by the orations that she gave at funerals, where people were entitled to stand up and speak of the doings of the deceased, friends had tried to persuade her to stand for the legislature, but she had declined, saying that she liked to talk about interesting things, and that there was never any talk of interesting things in Parliament.

"All they do is talk about money and roads and things like that," she had said. "Those are important things, and somebody has to talk about them, but let the men do that. We women have more important things to talk about."

"No, no, Mma.!" they said. "That is precisely the wrong attitude. That is what men want us to think. They want us to think that these important things they discuss are not really important to women. But they are! They are very important. And if we let the men talk about them and decide them, then suddenly we wake up and find out that the men have made all the decisions, and these decisions all suit men."

Mma. Boko had considered this carefully. "There is some truth in that," she had said. "In the bank the decisions were made by men. They did not ask me first."

"You see!" they said. "You see how it works. They are always doing this, the men. We women must stand up on our legs and talk."

Mma. Ramotswe examined the jam which Mma. Boko was making, and took the small spoonful which her friend offered her.

"It is good," she said. "This is the best jam in Botswana, I think."

Mma. Boko shook her head. "There are ladies here in Molepolole who make much better jam than this. I will bring you some of their jam one day, and you will see."

"I cannot believe it will be better," said Mma. Ramotswe, licking the spoon clean.

They sat down and talked. Mma. Boko told Mma. Ramotswe of her grandchildren, of whom she had sixteen. They were all clever, she said, although one of her daughters had married a rather unintelligent man. "He is kind, though," she said. "Even if he says very stupid things, he is kind."

Mma. Ramotswe told her about Mr. J.L.B. Matekoni's illness, and how he had been nursed back to health by Mma. Potokwani. She told her about the move to Tlokweng Road Speedy Motors and the sharing of the offices, and of how well he had been handled by Mma. Makutsi. She told her about the children; how Motholeli had been bullied and how Puso had been through a difficult patch.

"Boys do go through times like that," said Mma. Boko. "It can last for fifty years."

Then they talked about Molepolole and about the Botswana Rural Women's Association and about its plans. Eventually, after these multitudinous subjects had been exhausted, Mma. Ramotswe asked Mma. Boko the question which had brought her out on the visit.

"There is a girl," she began, "or was a girl—she is a woman now—called Tebogo Bathopi. About twenty years ago she came to Gaborone from Molepolole to train to be a nurse. I am not sure if she ever managed to finish—I do not think that she did. Something happened to her in Gaborone which somebody now wants to set right. I cannot tell you what that thing was, but I can tell you that the person involved is very serious about righting what he now sees was a wrong. He means it. But he does not know where this girl is. He has no idea. That is why I have come to you. You know everybody. You see everything. I thought you could help me to find out where this woman is, if she is still alive."

Mma. Boko laid down the spoon with which she had been stirring her jam.

"Of course she is still alive," she said, laughing. "Of course she is still alive. She is now called Mma. Tshenyego."

Mma. Ramotswe's surprise showed itself in a broad smile. She had not imagined that it would be this easy, but her instinct to ask Mma. Boko had proved correct. It was always the best way of finding out information; just go and ask a woman who keeps her eyes and ears open and who likes to talk. It always worked. It was no use asking men; they simply were not interested enough in other people and the ordinary doings of people. That is why the real historians of Africa had always been the grandmothers, who remembered the lineage and the stories that went with it.

"I am very glad to hear that, Mma.," she said. "Can you tell me where she is?"

"Over there," answered Mma. Boko. "She is right there. At

that house over there. Do you see it? And look, there she is herself, coming out of the house with one of the children, that girl,
who is sixteen now. That is her firstborn, her first daughter."

Mma. Ramotswe looked in the direction in which Mma.
Boko was pointing. She saw a woman coming out of the house,
together with a girl in a yellow dress. The woman threw some
grain to the chickens in the yard, and then they stood and
watched the chickens peck away at the food.

"She has many hens," said Mma. Boko, "and she is also one
of those ladies who makes good jam. She is always in that house,
cleaning and cooking and making things. She is a good person."

"So she did not become a nurse?" asked Mma. Ramotswe.

"No, she is not a nurse," said Mma. Boko. "But she is a clever
lady and she could have been a nurse. Maybe one of her daughters will become a nurse."

Mma. Ramotswe rose to take her leave.

"I must go and see that lady," she said to Mma. Boko. "But
first I must give you a present which I have brought for you. It is
in my van."

She walked over to the van and took out a parcel wrapped in
brown paper. This she gave to Mma. Boko, who unwrapped it and
saw that it contained a length of printed cotton, enough for a
dress. Mma. Boko held the material up against her.

"You are a very kind lady, Mma. Ramotswe," she said. "This
will be a very fine dress."

"And you are a useful friend," said Mma. Ramotswe.

CHAPTER EIGHTEEN

A RADIO IS A SMALL THING

MR. MOLEFELO arrived at the No. 1 Ladies' Detective Agency the following morning. Mma. Ramotswe had telephoned him the previous evening and had suggested an appointment in a few days' time, but such had been his eagerness to hear what she had found out that he begged her to see him sooner.

"Please, Mma.," he had pleaded. "I cannot wait. After all this time, I must know soon. Please do not make me wait. I shall be sitting here thinking, thinking, all the time."

There were other things that Mma. Ramotswe had to do, but these were not urgent and she understood his anxiety. So she agreed to see him at her office the next day when, she said, she would be able to give him the information he wanted. This required arrangements to be made, of course, and there was the older apprentice to dispatch on an errand. But that could be done.

Mr. Molefelo was punctual, waiting outside in his car until exactly eleven o'clock, the time at which Mma. Ramotswe had agreed to see him. Mma. Makutsi showed him into the office and then returned to her desk. Mr. Molefelo greeted Mma. Ramotswe and then looked at Mma. Makutsi.

"I wonder, Mma. . . ." he began.

Mma. Ramotswe caught Mma. Makutsi's eye, and that was enough. They both understood that there were things that could be said to one but not to two. And there were other reasons.

"I have to go to the post, Mma.," said Mma. Makutsi. "Should I go now?"

"A very good idea," said Mma. Ramotswe.

Mma. Makutsi left the office, throwing an injured look in Mr. Molefelo's direction, but he did not notice. As soon as she had left, Mr. Molefelo spoke.

"I must know, Mma.," he said, wringing his hands as he spoke. "I must know. Are they late? Are they late?"

"No, they are not late, Rra.," said Mma. Ramotswe. "Mr. Tsolamosese has died, but his widow is still alive. You came to me in time."

Mr. Molefelo's relief was palpable. "In that case, I can do what I need to do."

"Yes," said Mma. Ramotswe. "You can do what needs to be done." She paused. "I shall tell you first about Tebogo. I found her, you know."

Mr. Molefelo nodded eagerly. "Good. And . . . and what had happened to her? Was she well?"

"She was fine," said Mma. Ramotswe. "I found her in Molepolole, very easily. I drank tea with her and we talked. She told me about her life."

"I am. . . ." Mr. Molefelo tried to speak but found that he had nothing to say.

"She said that she did not train as a nurse after all. She was very upset when you made her deal with the baby in that way. She said that she cried and cried, and for many months she had bad dreams about what she had done."

"That was my fault," said Mr. Molefelo. "My fault."

"Yes it was," said Mma. Ramotswe. "But you were a young man then, weren't you? Young men do these things. It is only later that they regret them."

"It was wrong of me to say that she should end that baby. I know that."

Mma. Ramotswe looked at him. "It is not that simple, Rra. There are times when you cannot expect a woman to have a baby. It is not always right. Many women would tell you that."

"I am not questioning that," said Mr. Molefelo meekly. "I am just telling you what I feel."

"She was upset about you, too, you know," went on Mma. Ramotswe. "She said that she loved you and that you had told her that, too. Then you changed your mind, and she was very upset. She said that you had a hard heart."

Mr. Molefelo looked down at the floor. "It is true. I had a hard heart. . . ."

"But then she said that she met another boy and he asked her to marry him. He joined the police, and then later on he found a job as a bus driver. They live out at Molepolole, and they have been happy. They have five children. I met the oldest girl."

Mr. Molefelo listened attentively. "Is that all?" he said. "Is that all that happened? Did you tell her how sorry I was?"

"I did," said Mma. Ramotswe,

"And what did she say?"

"She said that you must not worry. She said that her life had turned out very well and she bore you no ill will. She said that she hoped that you had been happy, too." She paused. "I think that you wanted to help her in some way, didn't you, Rra.?"

Mr. Molefelo was smiling. "I said that, Mma., and I meant it. I want to give her some money."

"That might not be the best way to do it," said Mma. Ramotswe. "What do you think the husband of this woman would think if she received money from an old boyfriend? He might not like it at all."

"Then what can I do?"

"I met her daughter," said Mma. Ramotswe. "I told you that. She is a clever girl. She is the one who would like to be a nurse now. She is very keen. I spoke to her about it. But there are not many places for nurse training, and it is the girls who get the best results who will get the places."

"Is she clever?" asked Mr. Molefelo. "Her mother was clever."

"She is clever enough, I think," said Mma. Ramotswe. "But she would stand an even better chance if she went for a year or two to one of those schools where they charge high fees. They teach the children very carefully there. It would be a very good chance for her."

Mr. Molefelo was silent. "The fees are high," he said. "That costs a lot of money."

Mma. Ramotswe looked at him, meeting his gaze. "I do not think that you can make up for things cheaply, Rra. Do you?"

Mr. Molefelo looked at her, hesitated, and then he smiled. "You are a very astute lady, Mma., and I think you are right. I will pay for that girl to go to one of those schools here in Gaborone. I will pay that."

Half the medicine, thought Mma. Ramotswe. *Now for the other half.* She looked out of the window. The apprentice had left shortly before nine o'clock, and allowing for delays at the roundabouts and for one or two wrong turnings, he should be back very soon. She could start, though, by telling him of how she had found Mma. Tsolamosese.

"The father died," she said. "He retired from prison service and then he died. But Mma. Tsolamosese herself is well, and she is living on her widow's pension from the department. I think that she has enough. Her house seemed comfortable, and she is with her people. I think she is happy."

"That is very good," said Mr. Molefelo. "But was she also cross with me when you told her what had happened?"

"She was very surprised," said Mma. Ramotswe. "At first she did not believe that you could have done it. I had to persuade her that it was true. Then she said that she thought that you were very brave to confess what had happened. That's what she said."

Mr. Molefelo, who had looked cheerful before, now looked miserable again. "She must think I am very bad. She must think that I abused her hospitality. That is a very bad thing to do."

"She understands," said Mma. Ramotswe. "She is a woman who has lived quite a long time. She understands that young men can behave like that. Do not think that she is filled with anger, or anything like that."

"She is not?"

"No. And she is also happy that you should apologise in person. She is prepared for that."

"Then I must go out there," said Mr. Molefelo.

Mma. Ramotswe glanced out of her window. The tiny white van was being driven up to the back of the garage.

"No need to go out there, Rra.," she said. "Mma. Tsolamosese has just arrived. She will be here in a moment." She paused. "Are you all right, Rra.?"

Mr. Molefelo gulped. "I am very embarrassed, Mma. I feel very bad. But I think I am ready."

MMA. TSOLAMOSESE looked at the man standing before her.

"You are looking very well," she said. "You were thinner in those days. You were a boy."

"You were my mother, Mma. You looked after me well."

She smiled at him. "I was your mother in Gaborone. You were my son while you were here. Now I am proud of you. Mma. Ramotswe has told me how well you have done."

"But I did a very bad thing to you," said Mr. Molefelo. "Your radio—"

Mma. Tsolamosese interrupted him. "A radio is a small thing. A man is a big thing."

"I am sorry, Mma.," said Mr. Molefelo. "I am sorry for what I did. I have never stolen anything else. That was the only time."

"Do not worry, Rra.," she said. "I have told you already. A radio is a small thing."

They sat down together while Mma. Ramotswe prepared the tea. Then, over the strong, sweet liquid, they talked about what had happened in their lives. At the end of the conversation, Mma. Ramotswe drew Mr. Molefelo to one side and spoke to him quietly.

"There is something you can do for this woman," she said. "It will not cost you too much money, but it is something that you can do."

He glanced over his shoulder at Mma. Tsolamosese. "She is such a kind woman," he whispered. "She was like that then, and she still is. I will do whatever I can."

"There is a grandchild," said Mma. Ramotswe quietly. "There is a little girl. She may not live very long because of this cruel illness. But in the meantime, you could make a difference to that life. You could give Mma. Tsolamosese money to use for that child. The right food. Meat. Pretty clothes. Even if the life of that child is short, it would be made a happy one, and if you did that, Rra., then you would have more than made up for what you did all those years ago."

Mr. Molefelo looked at her. "You are right, Mma. I can do that. It is not a big thing to do."

"Then you tell Mma. Tsolamosese," said Mma. Ramotswe, gesturing towards the older woman. "You go ahead and tell her."

Mma. Tsolamosese listened quietly as Mr. Molefelo spoke. Then, her head bowed, she spoke.

"I always thought that you were a good person, Rra.," she said. "All those years ago, I thought that. Nothing that I have heard, nothing, has made me change my mind about you."

She looked up and reached for his hand, while Mma. Ramotswe turned away. Mr. Molefelo had earned this moment for himself, she thought, and there should be no spectator.

CHAPTER NINETEEN

NO. 42 LIMPOPO COURT

MR. MOLEFELO had written two cheques that day: one to Mma. Ramotswe, for her professional services (three thousand pula, a steep fee, but one which he was well able to afford), and another for two thousand pula, to be deposited in a post office savings account in the name of Mma. Tsolamosese, for the benefit of her grandchild. More cheques would need to be made out for school fees, but again, Mr. Molefelo had made a considerable amount of money, and these sums would not be noticed. In return, after all, as Mma. Ramotswe was at pains to explain to him, he had corrected the moral balance of his past and earned the right to an easy conscience.

But Mma. Ramotswe's sense of achievement was marred by the question brought to her attention by Mma. Selelipeng, the physiotherapist from Mochudi. Mma. Ramotswe would dearly have loved this issue to have gone away, but it remained stubbornly present and would have to be dealt with. At least she had now decided what to do; she had Mr. Bernard Selelipeng's address right there in her hand, and she would go and see him early that evening, shortly after he arrived home from work.

She knew Limpopo Court, a newish block of flats near Tlokweng Road. She had been in one of the flats there before, visiting a distant cousin, and its shape and its stuffiness had discouraged her. Mma. Ramotswe liked the old round shapes of traditional architecture; hard edges and sharp roofs struck her as being unfriendly and uncomfortable. And a traditional house *smelled* better, because there was no concrete, which has such a bad odour, dank and acrid. A traditional house smelled of wood smoke, the earth, and of thatch; all good smells, the smell of life itself.

No. 42 was on the first floor, reached by an ugly concrete walkway that ran the length of the building. She glanced at the door, with its shiny blue paint, and at the name, Selelipeng, which had been stencilled on it in pride of ownership. She felt unhappy and concerned, even anxious; what she had to do was not easy, but she could see no way out of it. She had agreed to act on behalf of Mma. Selelipeng, and she could not go back on her word. At the same time, she was aware of the fact that she was interfering in Mma. Makutsi's affairs in a way to which her employee might object. Would she, were she in the shoes of Mma. Makutsi, want her employer meddling in a romance which clearly meant so much to her? She thought not. But then were she in Mma. Makutsi's position, she would not have to worry about the obligation she owed to Mma. Selelipeng. So it was not as simple as Mma. Makutsi might imagine.

Unaware of the moral quandary which he had created for Mma. Ramotswe, Mr. Bernard Selelipeng, his tie loosened after a demanding day in the diamond office, opened the door to Mma. Ramotswe's knock. He saw before him a large, well-built lady, vaguely familiar to him in some context. Who was she? A relative? Cousins of cousins were always appearing on his doorstep wanting something. At least this woman did not look hungry.

"Mr. Selelipeng?"

"My name is on the door, Mma."

Mma. Ramotswe smiled at him. She saw the centre parting and the expensive blue shirt. She noticed the shoes, which were shinier than the shoes that most men wore.

"I have to speak to you, Rra., about an important matter. Please, will you invite me in?"

Mr. Selelipeng drew back from the door, gesturing for Mma. Ramotswe to enter. Pointing to a chair, he invited her to sit down.

"I am not sure who you are, Mma.," he began. "I think I have met you, but I am sorry, I am not sure."

"I am Precious Ramotswe," she said. "I am the owner of the No. 1 Ladies' Detective Agency. You may have heard of us."

Mr. Selelipeng looked surprised. "I have heard of your agency," he said. "There was an interview in the newspaper the other day."

Mma. Ramotswe bit her lip. "That was not us, Rra.. That was another business. Nothing to do with us." She made an effort to keep the irritation out of her voice, but she was afraid that it showed, as Mr. Selelipeng seemed to become tense as she spoke.

"The No. 1 Ladies' Detective Agency," went on Mma. Ramotswe, "is run by two women. There is me—I am the manager—and there is a lady who works for me as assistant detective. She is a person who came from the Botswana Secretarial College and is now working for me. I think you know her."

Mr. Selelipeng said nothing.

"She is called Mma. Makutsi," said Mma. Ramotswe. "That is the name of this lady."

Mr. Selelipeng did not lower his eyes, but Mma. Ramotswe noticed that he was no longer smiling. She noticed how he was drumming the fingers of his right hand on the arm of his chair, His other hand lay on his lap but was slightly clenched, she saw.

Mma. Ramotswe took a deep breath. "I know that you are seeing this lady, Rra. She has spoken of you."

Still Mr. Selelipeng said nothing.

"She was very happy when you invited her out," she continued. "I could tell from the way that she was behaving that something good was happening in her life. And then she mentioned your name. She said—"

Suddenly Mr. Selelipeng interrupted. "So," he said, his voice raised. "So what has this got to do with you, Mma.? I don't like to be rude, but is this any of your business? You are her boss, but you do not own her life, do you?"

Mma. Ramotswe sighed. "I can understand how you feel, Rra. I can imagine that you think I am a busybody woman who is trying to put her nose into matters that do not concern her."

"Well?" said Mr. Selelipeng. "There, you have said it yourself. You yourself have said that it is only a busybody who talks about these things, like some old woman in a village, watching, watching."

"I am only doing what I have to do, Rra.," said Mma. Ramotswe defensively.

"Hah! Why do you have to do this? Why do you have to come and talk to me about this private matter? You tell me that."

"Because your wife asked me to," said Mma. Ramotswe quietly. "That is why."

Her words had the effect that she had thought they would. Mr. Selelipeng opened his mouth, and then he closed it. He swallowed. Then he opened his mouth again, and Mma. Ramotswe saw that he had a gold cap on a tooth slightly to the right side. His mouth closed.

"You are worried, Rra.? Did you not tell Mma. Makutsi that you were a married man?"

Mr. Selelipeng now seemed crumpled. He had moved back slightly in his chair, and his shoulders had slumped.

"I was going to tell her," he said lamely. "I was going to tell her, but I had not got round to it yet. I am very sorry."

Mma. Ramotswe looked into his eyes and saw the lie. This did not surprise her; indeed, Mr. Selelipeng had behaved true to form and had not caused her to rethink her strategy in any way. It would have been different, of course, if he had laughed when she mentioned his wife, but he had not done that. This was not a man who was going to leave his wife; that was very apparent.

She now had the advantage. "So, Mr. Selelipeng, what do you think we should do about this? Your wife has instructed me to report on your activities. I have a professional duty to her. I also have to think about the interests of my employee, Mma. Makutsi. I do not want her to be hurt . . . by a man who has no intention of staying with her."

At this, Mr. Selelipeng made an attempt to glower at her, but she met his gaze and held it, and he wilted.

"Please do not tell my wife about this, Mma.," he said, his voice thin and pleading. "I am sorry that I have inconvenienced Mma. Makutsi. I do not want to hurt her."

"Perhaps you should have thought about that earlier, Rra. Perhaps you should have . . ." She stopped herself. She was a kind woman, and the sight of this man, so wretched and fearful, made it difficult for her to say anything to exacerbate his discomfort. *I could never be a judge,* she thought; *I could not sit there and punish people after they have begun to feel sorry for what they have done.*

"We could try to sort this out," she said. "We could try to make sure that Mma. Makutsi is not too badly upset. In particular, Rra., I do not want her to think that she has been thrown over . . . thrown over by somebody who no longer loves her. And I do not want her to find out that she has been seeing a married man. That would make her feel bad about herself, which is what I definitely do not want to happen. Do you understand me?"

Mr. Selelipeng nodded eagerly. "I will do what you tell me to do, Mma."

"I thought, Rra., that it might be better if you were to move back to Mochudi for a while. You could tell Mma. Makutsi that you have to go away and that you are not giving her up because you do not love her. Then you must tell her that you do not think that you are worthy of her, even if you are still in love with her. Then you will buy her a very fine present and some flowers. You will know what to do. But you must make sure that she is not being thrown away. That would be very bad, and I would find it difficult then not to talk to your wife about all this. Do you understand me?"

"I understand you very well," said Mr. Selelipeng. "You can be sure that I will try to make it easy for her."

"That is what you must do, Rra."

She rose to her feet, preparing to leave.

"And another thing, Rra.," she said. "I would like you to remember that in the future these things may not work out quite so easily for you. Bear that in mind."

"There is not going to be a next time," said Mr. Bernard Selelipeng.

BUT AS she made her way back to the tiny white van, he was watching from his window, and he thought: *I have no happiness now. I am just a man who provides for that woman and her children. She does not love me, but she will not let me find somebody who does love me. And I am too much of a coward to walk away and tell her that I have my own life, which will soon be gone anyway, because I am getting older. And now I no longer have that lady, who was so good to me. One day I will put a stop to all this. One day.*

And Mma. Ramotswe, glancing up, saw him at his window before he retreated, and she thought: *Poor man! It could have been different for him, if he had not lied to Mma. Makutsi. Why is it that there are always these problems and misunderstandings between men and women? Surely it would have been better if God had made only one sort of person, and the children had come by some other means, with the rain, perhaps.*

She thought about this as she started the van and began to drive away. But if there were only one sort of person, would this person be more like a man than a woman? The answer was obvious, thought Mma. Ramotswe. One hardly even had to think about it.

CHAPTER TWENTY

TWO AWKWARD MEN
SATISFACTORILY DISPOSED OF

I T SEEMED to Mma. Ramotswe that the run of misfortune that had begun with the illness of Mr. J.L.B. Matekoni, and which had continued through events such as the foreshortened affair of Mma. Makutsi with Mr. Bernard Selelipeng and the establishing of the rival agency, was now coming to an end. She had still been concerned about the Selelipeng matter, but she need not have been. Shortly after Mma. Ramotswe's visit to No. 42, Limpopo Court, Mma. Makutsi explained to her, quite spontaneously, that Mr. Selelipeng had unfortunately been called back to look after aged relatives in Mochudi. As a result of this, he was, most regrettably of course, not in a position to see her as regularly as he might have wished.

"A bit of a relief," she said. "I liked him to begin with, but then, you know how it is, Mma., I rather went off him."

For a moment Mma. Ramotswe's composure deserted her.

"You went off. . . . You. . . ."

"I was bored with him," said Mma. Makutsi airily. "He was a very nice man in many ways, but he was a bit too concerned about his appearance. He also just sat there and smiled at me all the time. He was definitely in love with me, which is nice, but you can get a bit bored with that sort of thing, can't you?"

"Of course," said Mma. Ramotswe hurriedly.

"He would just sit there and look into my eyes," went on Mma. Makutsi. "After a while, it made me go cross-eyed."

Mma. Ramotswe laughed. "Some girls would like a man like that."

"Perhaps," said Mma. Makutsi. "But then, I'm looking for somebody with a bit more. . . ."

"Intelligence?"

"Yes."

"You are very wise," said Mma. Ramotswe.

Mma. Makutsi threw a hand in the air, as might one who could have her pick of men. "When he said that he was going off to Mochudi, I was very pleased. I said immediately that it would not be easy for us to see one another anymore and that perhaps it was best to say good-bye. He seemed surprised, but I tried to make it easy for him. So we agreed on that. He gave me a very nice present, too. A necklace with a very small diamond in it. He said that he could get them at a special price from the company."

She took a silver chain out of a small packet and showed it to Mma. Ramotswe. Suspended on the chain was a small chip of diamond, almost invisible. He could have been more generous, thought Mma. Ramotswe, but at least he did it, which was the important thing.

Mma. Ramotswe looked at Mma. Makutsi. She wondered whether she was putting a brave face on it, or whether she really had been intending to get rid of Mr. Bernard Selelipeng. No, there was only one possibility. Mma. Makutsi was a scrupulously truthful person, and she would not—she could not—sit there and tell Mma. Ramotswe a skein of lies. So she had made the first move after all. It was astonishing how life had a way of working out, even when everything looked so complicated and unpromising.

EVEN MORE astonishing, though, was the arrival later that day of Mr. Buthelezi, who knocked on the door, entered uninvited, and cheerfully extended a greeting to both Mma. Ramotswe and Mma. Makutsi.

"So this is your place," he said, looking about the office with a rather condescending air. "I wondered what sort of office you ladies would have. I thought there might be more feminine things. Curtains, you know, things like that."

Mma. Ramotswe looked at Mma. Makutsi. If there was a limit to this man's nerve, then they had yet to plumb it.

"You people are very busy, I hear," he said. "Lots of cases. This and that."

"Yes," said Mma. Ramotswe, adding: "Some clients even came from—"

"Oh, I know about that," said Mr. Buthelezi. "That woman! I told her the truth, I told—"

Mma. Ramotswe coughed loudly. She had inadvertently mentioned Mma. Selelipeng, forgetting for a moment the careful steps she had taken to prevent Mma. Makutsi from hearing anything about it. "Yes, yes, Rra. Let's forget all about that. It was nothing. Now, what can we do for you today? Do you need a detective?"

At this Mma. Makutsi burst out laughing but was silenced by a look from Mr. Buthelezi.

"Very funny, Mma.," he said. "The truth of the matter is that you can keep the detective business. I have had enough of it. I do not think it is the right business for me."

For a moment Mma. Ramotswe was speechless. It was true: the natural order was indeed restoring itself after all these setbacks.

"It's a very boring business, I've decided," said Mr. Buthelezi. "This is a small town. People in this place lead very boring lives. They have no problems to sort out. It is not like Johannesburg."

"Or New York?" interjected Mma. Makutsi.

"Yes," said Mr. Buthelezi. "It is not like New York, either."

"So what are you going to do, Rra.?" asked Mma. Ramotswe. "Are you going to find another business?"

"I'll try to think of something," said Mr. Buthelezi. "Something will turn up."

"What about a driving school?" asked Mma. Makutsi. "You would be good at that."

Mr. Buthelezi spun round to face Mma. Makutsi's desk. "That is a very good idea, Mma. It is a very good idea. My, my! You are a clever lady. Not just beautiful but clever, too."

"You could call it LEARN TO DRIVE WITH JESUS," Mma. Makutsi suggested. "You would get many safe, religious people coming to you."

"Hah!" said Mr. Buthelezi, his voice raised. And then, "Hah!" again.

They have such loud voices, these people, thought Mma. Ramotswe; *they are all like that. They just are.*

THE FOLLOWING week, because life now seemed to be more ordered and satisfactory, Mma. Ramotswe, Mma. Makutsi, and Mr. J.L.B. Matekoni organised a gathering by the side of the dam. Not only did they invite the two apprentices, but they also asked Mma. Potokwani and her husband, Mma. Boko, who was fetched from Molepolole by one of the apprentices, and Mr. Molefelo and his family. Mma. Ramotswe and Mma. Makutsi worked hard at preparing fried chicken and sausages, together with ample quantities of rice and maize pap. At the picnic itself, the apprentices made a small fire on which thick slices of beef were grilled.

There were other groups picnicking there at the same time, including several families with teenage girls. The apprentices soon started talking to these girls and sat on a rock away from the others, exchanging jokes and conversation of a sort which Mr. J.L.B. Matekoni could only imagine.

"What do these young people talk about?" he said to Mma. Ramotswe. "Just look at them. Even the religious one is talking to those girls and trying to touch them on the arm."

"He has gone back to girls," said Mma. Makutsi, picking up a tempting bit of chicken and popping it into her mouth. "I have noticed that. He will not be religious for long."

"I thought that might happen," said Mma. Ramotswe. "People do not change all that much."

She looked at Mr. J.L.B. Matekoni, who was poking at a piece of meat on the fire. It was good that people did not change, except, she supposed, where there was room for improvement. Mr. J.L.B. Matekoni was perfect as he was, she thought; a good man, with a profound feeling for machinery and possessed of a nature made up of utter kindness. There were so few men like that around; how satisfactory it was, then, that she had one of them.

Mma. Potokwani filled a plate with chicken and rice and passed it to her husband.

"How fortunate we are," she said. "How fortunate that we have been given these kind friends, and that we are living in this place, which is so good to us. We are lucky people."

"We are," echoed her husband, who agreed with everything his wife said, without exception.

"Mma. Potokwani," said Mr. J.L.B. Matekoni, "is that new pump of yours working well?"

"Very well," said Mma. Potokwani. "But one of the house-mothers says that the hot-water system in her house is making a gurgling noise. I was wondering—"

"I will come and fix it," said Mr. J.L.B. Marekoni. "I will come tomorrow."

Mma. Ramotswe smiled, but only to herself.

africa
africa africa
africa africa africa
africa africa
africa